Margare[...]

Watch out for Elvis

in this book!

Are You Smarter Than A Flying Gator?

Gator Mikey Over Florida!

You're

awesome!

☺ Kevin Kremer

Other books by Kevin Kremer:

A Kremer Christmas Miracle

Spaceship Over North Dakota

Saved by Custer's Ghost

The Blizzard of the Millennium

When it Snows in Sarasota

Santa's Our Substitute Teacher

Are You Smarter Than A Than A Flying Gator?

Gator Mikey Over Florida!

by Kevin Kremer

Illustrated by Dave Ely

Published by Snow in Sarasota Publishing
2007
P.O. Box 1360
Osprey, FL 34229-1360
www.snowinsarasota.com

Snow in Sarasota Publishing
P.O. Box 1360
Osprey, FL 34229-1360

Visit us on the Web! www.snowinsarasota.com

ISBN-10: 0-9663335-6-X
ISBN-13: 978-0-9663335-6-5

Library of Congress Control Number: 2007908791

Printed in the United States of America

10 9 8 7 6 5 4 3 2 1

First Edition

PUBLISHER'S NOTE

This book is dedicated to
Mom and Dad.
You're the best!

Esto
Two Egg
Niceville
Pensacola
Panama City

Florida

Quincy
• Tallahassee
• St. Marks
Lake City
Jacksonville
St. Augustine •
Bald Point
State Park
Gainesville
Cedar Key
Ocala
Daytona Beach
27
Umatilla
Kennedy Space Center
Zephyrhills
Haines City
Plant City
Dunedin
Tampa
St. Petersburg
Anna Maria
Island
Bradenton
Sarasota
Sebring Raceway
Siesta Key
Venice
Port Charlotte
GATORAMA
Ft. Meyers
Lake
Okeechobee
27
Naples
Alligator Alley
Ft. Lauderdale
Miami
Miami International
Airport
Key West

PROLOGUE

You've probably already heard about Prez and his eight friends who call themselves *Sarabiskota*. Those were the kids in the news last summer who found that big treasure chest at the bottom of the sea filled with gold coins, silver, sapphires, pearls, diamonds, and jewelry. It was all worth hundreds of millions of dollars!

If you've forgotten the story, let me refresh your memory a little. It involved those nine friends I referred to earlier. All of them had just finished the seventh grade. Their names were Jan Jones, Kari Wise, Katy Heidebrink, Jessie Angel, Chad Renner, Mike Schafer, Nick Hillman, Kevin Feeney, and Prez. With the exception of Katy, all of these close friends had grown up together in Bismarck, North Dakota.

This was definitely a bunch of precocious teens, but Prez brought new meaning to the word *precocious.* His brain was like an enormous sponge.

He loved learning, exploring, and inventing. At times Prez could be a little scatterbrained but that was quite understandable. His brain was usually working on so many things at the same time.

Prez was born in Bismarck with the name Mike Gold. After doing a report on Teddy Roosevelt in the second grade, Mike told his teacher he wanted to be President of the United States someday, just like Teddy. After that, some of Mike's friends started to call him *Prez* and the nickname stuck.

Last summer, Prez and his parents moved from Bismarck to Sarasota, Florida. At the time, Prez's dad's software company won a big military contract from Central Command in Tampa, and Prez's dad decided to relocate his company to the Tampa Bay area. Eventually, he chose to move it to Sarasota, which was a short distance to the south of Tampa Bay.

Although Prez had loved living in Bismarck his whole life, and he knew he'd miss his friends from Bismarck a lot, the move to Sarasota was made much easier because Chad Renner moved there with him. You see, Chad's parents both worked for Prez's dad. In fact, their two families had been good friends for a long time.

Making things even better, Prez's and Chad's families found new beach homes on the same block on the north end of one of the most beautiful islands in the world, Siesta Key. There was only one house between Prez's and Chad's.

The boys were pleasantly surprised when they found out who lived in that house. It turned out to be a cute, blonde girl the same age as the two boys. She had recently moved to Sarasota from Fergus Falls, Minnesota.

This was Katy Heidebrink, who the two boys soon nicknamed *KT*. KT's parents had bought a jet ski, bicycle, boat, kayak, and parasailing business on Siesta Key called Siesta Key Water Fun. Prez developed a big crush on KT the first time he saw her.

Not long after Chad and Prez met KT, the three teens wanted to find out if it had ever snowed in Sarasota on Christmas so they headed to the Selby Public Library in Sarasota to find out. While they were doing their research at the library, they stumbled upon a strange mystery involving a man known as Captain Sarasota who had mysteriously disappeared from his fishing boat out on Sarasota Bay a few years earlier. Captain Sarasota had left just one clue behind, which nobody had ever been able to figure out. It was a number carved into the wooden steering wheel of his fishing boat—487699.

KT, Chad, and Prez immediately became obsessed with trying to solve this mystery. With the help of their six other friends back in Bismarck, they eventually solved the mystery and it led them to the treasure worth all that money.

Somewhere along the way, the nine teens started to call themselves *Sarabiskota*. The *Sara* part comes from Sarasota, *bis* comes from Bismarck, the *k* comes from North Dakota, and *ota* comes from Sarasota, Minnesota, and North Dakota.

Now, I'll bet you remember the whole story. Just in case you get the nine Sarabiskota teenagers mixed up, I'll tell you a little more about each of them, starting with the girls.

Jan Jones — Jan's friends call her Doc because she wants to be a medical doctor someday. She even carries a medical book around with her a lot. Doc's super-smart and very funny. She has long brown hair and wears glasses. Doc plays the clarinet and her favorite sport is basketball.

Kari Wise — Kari's the tallest of the girls. She has short brown hair. She's a soccer player and an ice skater. Kari's an amazing organizer. After college, she's thinking about being a researcher of some kind and possibly starting her own research business. Kari plays the flute.

Jessie Angel — Jessie's last name applies, or at least she has a guardian angel. You see, Jessie and her mom were riding in a car over a bridge near their home south of Bismarck when the bridge collapsed. Their car fell down into the river below, but they got out without even a scratch. Everyone thought it was a miracle. Jessie has very light blonde hair. She's artistic and really funny. She's also an excellent competitive swimmer and likes to play the saxophone.

KT — Besides what you already know about KT, I could add that her favorite sports are volleyball and track. KT's not sure what she wants to study when she goes to college, but she really likes working with young children.

Chad Renner — Chad's a natural all-around athlete.

He's probably most talented at freestyle wrestling. Chad's tall with short black hair. He likes to play the trumpet, but he doesn't seem to find much time to practice playing it.

Mike Schafer — Mike looks a lot like a young Elvis Presley and loves to talk and sing like Elvis. That's right. He's an Elvis impersonator and he's really good at it. Besides that, Mike loves cross country running, the long jump, and playing his drums.

Nick Hillman — Nick asks tons of questions when he doesn't understand something. He loves to play hockey and football, and he's really good at both sports. Nick's a NASCAR fanatic and a huge University of Minnesota hockey fan. Nick is almost Chad's height with short brown hair.

Kevin Feeney — Kevin is the shortest of the group, but he's really strong. He has short, black, straight hair. Kevin is a talented quarterback for his age, and he wants to keep growing and become the University of Nebraska Cornhuskers' quarterback someday. He may be the biggest sports fanatic of the whole group.

Prez — Prez is not ashamed to tell people that he had a weight problem when he was younger. Over the years his friends have helped encourage him to eat better and get involved in sports. It's made a huge difference. Prez has slimmed down a lot, and he's even become a pretty good athlete. This past year he played football at his middle school in Sarasota. Prez has short, dark, curly hair. He's about four inches shorter than Chad. Prez likes to play the violin.

The nine friends who called themselves Sarabiskota couldn't wait for the summer to arrive. After all, their parents were giving them the greatest gift imaginable: they were allowing them to spend the entire summer together on Siesta Key in Sarasota, Florida.

Doc, Kari, Jessie, Mike, Nick, and Kevin had to get up really early on Saturday, May 30, to catch their 7:00 a.m. flight from Bismarck to Minneapolis. From Minneapolis they had to fly to Atlanta, and from there, to Sarasota.

When the Bismarck travelers were changing flights in Atlanta, Jessie called Prez.

"Hey, Prez. We're switching planes in Atlanta already. Are you on the way to your airport yet?"

"Don't worry, Jessie. My mom, KT, Chad, and I are leaving pretty soon. We'll be there way before you land."

Kari grabbed the cell phone from Jessie. "Prez, do we have time for a long boat ride today?"

"Plenty of time, Kari," Prez replied. "I have a little

something I'd like to discuss with all of you anyway. The boat ride would be a good time to do that."

"Prez, do you already have something cooking up in that huge brain of yours?" Kari asked.

"Yup."

"Cool," said Kari. "Hey, Prez. I know I shouldn't worry about stuff, but that's what I like to do. How are we all going to get around this summer?"

"I assume you mean transportation arrangements. We've got it all under control, Kari. With all the water around Sarasota, my boat can get us just about anywhere. For our special terrestrial transportation needs, Chad's parents and my parents have rented an extended van. When you want to get a little exercise, KT's parents are letting each of us use a bicycle from their store."

"Fabulous," Kari said. "Sounds like you have everything covered."

"I think so. I'll see you on the ground soon."

"I can't wait!"

"Oh, Kari. Could you let me talk to Nick for a second?"

"Sure."

Kari handed Jessie's cell phone to Nick.

"Hi Prez. What's up?"

"I forgot to tell you before, Nick. KT, Chad, and I even bought you a special night light. We know how much you like your night lights."

"You guys are the greatest! Uh ... is it a Jeffie Gordon #24 NASCAR night light?"

"Oh, my gosh! You're psychic, Nick!"

"No, actually KT already sent me a text message about that."

There were lots of hugs, giggles, and talking after the plane landed at the Sarasota-Bradenton International Airport and the nine friends were reunited in the airport terminal. Once they retrieved their luggage, they loaded the van and headed back to Siesta Key.

As they were riding down U.S. Highway 41, several black bugs smashed into the windshield of the van. "What are those?" Kevin asked.

"They're called love bugs because the boy and girl bugs like to fly around together," Chad replied. "They're a real nuisance. We get zillions of them flying around twice a year."

"They were much worse a few days ago," KT added. "I think they're declining in numbers."

"They look a lot like box elder bugs," Doc

11

noted.

"They sure do," said Prez. "They also make a mess out of the cars around here, but we get used to them."

"Hey, what do you kids have planned for the rest of the day?" Mrs. Gold asked.

"I think we're going for a long boat ride, Mom," Prez answered. "It's Kari's special request."

"Sounds like fun," said Mrs. Gold. "I'd like you all back on land before seven if possible. We're going to have a little *welcome Sarabiskota barbecue* on the beach."

"Sounds great, Mrs. Gold!" Kevin said excitedly.

Jessie giggled. "Mrs. Gold, you don't have to spoil us like this, but if you choose to, it's fine with me."

Everyone laughed.

"It's so much fun having all of you together down here in Florida," Mrs. Gold said cheerfully. "Now, Mike, I wonder if you could do me a big favor."

"Sure, Mrs. Gold," Mike replied.

"Would you mind singing one of my favorite Elvis songs on the way back to Siesta Key?"

"That's easy. Which song would you like me to

13

sing?"

"Would you sing my favorite, 'Heartbreak Hotel'?"

"No problem."

Mike suddenly changed his facial expression, moved his lips around a little and started to get into his Elvis Presley state of mind. Then, in a voice that sounded just like Elvis, Mike said, "Thank you. Thank you very much for allowing all of us to be here in lovely Sarasota, Mrs. Gold. Now, I'd like to sing one of my most popular songs, 'Heartbreak Hotel,' with slight modifications ..."

Well, since I left Bismarck,
    I found a new place to dwell,
It's down by the Gulf of Mexico,
    At Siesta Key Hotel ...

A warm and enthusiastic welcome awaited them as they pulled into the Golds' driveway on Siesta Key. KT's parents, Chad's parents, Prez's dad, and Prez's little brother and sister were all there to greet them.

There was a large **Welcome Sarabiskota Girls** banner on the front of KT's house. The girls were all staying together there the whole summer.

On Chad's house there was a large banner that read **Welcome to the Sarabiskota Boys' Dormitory.** The boys were all staying at Chad's house.

There was a banner on Prez's house that proclaimed **Breakfast Served at 7:30 a.m.** It had been decided that Sarabiskota could eat breakfast together every morning at the Golds' house. They had a huge kitchen.

It didn't take long for everyone to unload the van and carry all the luggage into the houses. After that, the nine teens quickly changed into their swimming suits.

Soon all of them were sitting comfortably in the 37-foot boat Prez had named the *Rough Rider* in honor of his favorite President, Teddy Roosevelt. There was an obvious problem, though. The boat was still on its trailer in the Gold's driveway next to the van more than 30 yards from the beach. Besides that, the trailer wasn't attached to a car or truck. These facts, however, didn't seem to faze Sarabiskota one bit.

"May I push the buttons, Prez?" Nick asked eagerly.

Prez casually reached into his swimsuit's front pocket, pulled out a small remote control device, and handed it to Nick.

"Sure, Nick," Prez replied. "Press the *one* button first, then the *nine*."

After Nick pressed the two buttons, there was the sound of a small engine. Soon, the trailer and boat were moving slowly in reverse toward the beach. When the trailer got to the edge of the water, Prez said, "Now press the *seven* button and hand me the remote control."

Nick pressed the seven button and they stopped. He handed the remote control to Prez.

"Will you teach me how to do the rest this summer?" Nick asked.

"You bet, Nick," Prez answered. "It's easy."

Prez pushed another button and the boat slowly rose approximately a foot above the trailer like it was a hovercraft. Next, he used a small joystick to guide the *Rough Rider* over deep enough water. Then, he slowly lowered the boat to the water's surface.

"That is *so* cool!" said Kevin.

"No doubt," Kari added. "It's got to be one of your best inventions *ever.*"

"Thanks," said Prez with a mischievous smile on his face. "But I think I have something in mind that will make this invention appear almost trivial."

All eyes turned in Prez's direction. He definitely had everyone's attention. "We'll talk about it on the way," Prez told his curious friends.

Prez started the boat's three 250-horsepower outboard motors, and soon the *Rough Rider* was traveling north in the beautiful, calm, sparkling blue waters off Siesta Key.

After a few minutes, Doc couldn't wait any longer. "What's going on, Prez?" she asked.

"Yeah, what's the deal?" said Kevin.

"Last week," Prez explained, "KT, Chad, and I

had a little experience on our last day of school that gave me an idea."

KT and Chad were nodding and smiling.

"It's huge, you guys!" exclaimed Chad.

"It's humongous!" added KT, as she ran her fingers through her hair where a love bug had just landed. The love bug flew away.

Prez said, "We'll stop at a small island up north a few miles and I'll show you what we're talking about. KT, Chad, and I like to hang out there."

Chad smirked. "KT and Prez named the island *Chad's Lost Flip Flop Island* because I lost a flip flop when we were on the island the first time—and we never found it."

Jessie got a sad look on her face. "A lost flip flop. That's *so* tragic," she said, looking gloomy for a few more seconds then cracking a big smile and laughing.

Doc tried to sound serious. "Chad, we can look for your lost flip flop when we get there if you'd like."

"That's all right. I've gotten over it," Chad said, making a face at his friends. "Besides that, I'm afraid you guys would come up with another ridiculous *new* name for the island like *Chad Lost His Flip Flop*

But Now It's Been Found Island. It's just too much for me to remember."

"Me too," said Nick. "I like the name Chad's Lost Flip Flop Island."

"Me three," added Mike.

Kevin giggled. "Me, three and a half."

Prez sped up and they headed through Big Pass. Minutes later, they had to slow down again as they passed under the Ringling Bridge and traveled out into Sarasota Bay. After that, they traveled north along Longboat Key for ten minutes until they approached Chad's Lost Flip Flop Island.

"Land ahoy!" called Kari.

"We'll drop anchor in the shallow water off that small beach up there," said Prez, pointing.

After they were anchored, Prez grabbed his portable DVD player. They all walked ashore in water barely knee deep. Once ashore, they walked nearby to an open area surrounded by trees.

Prez set his DVD player on a tree stump. As everyone gathered around, Prez explained, "This is what we watched on TV in school last week. It's the governor of Florida speaking to all the students and teachers in the state."

Prez pressed the *play* button.

"Good morning students and teachers in Florida. I'm Governor Charlie Trust, the governor of this great state. I feel so privileged to be able to speak to all of you this special morning, the last day of school for many of you.

"I'd like to talk to you about a special challenge. It's a challenge that any of you can start working on—maybe even use a portion of your precious summer vacation.

"Before I do that, let me say I'm very proud of your improvement on our state achievement test, the F-DOG. I know many of you don't like tests like this. They're tough and they make you very nervous. But Florida schools have made excellent gains in the past several years in math, reading, writing, and science. That's partly because of the F-DOG, but mostly because of your hard work.

"Also, we recently added physical education to all of our public elementary schools. You've been exercising and getting in better shape, and that's extremely important for you as young Floridians.

"Now, I'd like to help you lead an effort in some other important subject areas that we may be neglecting here in Florida. Think for a few moments about what those might be.

"Let me give you some hints. A study that came out last month revealed that fewer than half of all Floridians know the name of our country's Vice President. Sadly, only about one third of all Floridians know the name of their governor—that's me, Charlie Trust. Only one fourth know the European explorer who discovered Florida. Only about one out of ten know the states that border Florida. Would you believe only one out of 20 know how many amendments there are to the U.S. Constitution or how their own hometown got its name?

"You've probably guessed by now what subject areas we need to work on. I think we need to be focusing more on teaching and learning *geography* and *history* here in Florida. Beyond that, somehow we need to get all Floridians involved, not just those in school.

"How can you help? Well, I'm asking all of you to spend some time—maybe even part of your summer—on this special challenge. Begin thinking of ideas and projects that promote history and geography in our state. It would be fantastic if some of your ideas would involve not only those in your school, but everyone in your towns, counties, and possibly the whole state.

"Starting next fall, we'll have a special web site set up to share our ideas. Also, newspapers, television, and radio stations will be highlighting some of your ideas beginning next fall.

"I'll be speaking to you all again in August with further details about this. At that time, I'll also tell you about some of the great prizes we'll be offering for your ideas. Thank you for your time and have a fun and safe summer!"

Prez pressed the *stop* button. Then he got a huge grin on his face.

Kari asked, "Prez, what exactly do you have in mind?"

"It's big, isn't it?" asked Kevin.

"It's huge!" said Chad.

"Actually, it will be about 40 feet in length," said Prez, still smiling.

"I have a feeling we're going to be busy this summer," Mike said, anxious to find out what was percolating in Prez's gigantic brain.

"Time to share some details with us," Doc insisted.

"All right," said Prez. "This is what I have in mind, but it would mean *tons* of work on your part this summer ..."

When they returned to Siesta Key from their excursion to Chad's Lost Flip Flop Island, a wonderful beach barbecue awaited them. KT's dad and Chad's dad grilled steaks on one grill while Prez's dad cooked his special diced potatoes and corn on the cob on another grill. KT's, Prez's, and Chad's moms prepared some great salads and got the tables ready. Everyone sat comfortably around three picnic tables set end to end as they ate.

"What a beautiful place for a picnic!" Jessie said, bubbling with enthusiasm. "Parents, thanks for all of this."

"It's so awesome being here in Sarasota!" Kari added. "Thank you, parents, for letting us all be together here this summer."

"Thanks, parents. This is the greatest!" said Doc.

"Thank you. Thank you very much," Mike said in his Elvis Presley voice. Then, in his normal voice he added, "I love being in Sarasota."

"You're all very welcome," Mrs. Heidebrink said. "You know you're all like family to us anyway. I just hope none of you get homesick being away from your families for the whole summer."

"No problem," said Jessie. "My family's coming down here for part of their vacation in July just in case."

Kevin had lots of brothers and sisters. "Heck, my mom probably won't even know I'm missing until July," he said.

Everyone laughed.

Nick said, "We're going to be so busy and having so much fun—none of us will have time to get homesick."

Mr. Renner spoke up. "I know I speak on behalf of all the parents here who trust you and love you a lot ... please have a great time but keep us informed."

"We will," Kari assured them.

Prez's dad looked across the table at his son. "Prez, you guys already have something big on your agenda, don't you?"

"Actually ... yes, Dad. We were just talking about that on our boat ride."

"Is there anything you'd like to share with us *old* folks at this point?" Mr. Gold inquired.

"If you don't mind, we're going to make it a big surprise," Prez replied. "If it turns out the way we anticipate, it could be pretty amazing."

Prez's dad looked a little concerned. "Uh ... do you have any idea how much time and expense might be involved?"

Prez thought a few seconds. "Time frame ... we want to be finished with the project before everyone has to head back to Bismarck in early August," he said. "Money? There's no way to tell at this point, but I think I've already got most of the materials we need in the workshop. If we have any significant expenses at all, I'll let you know."

Chad's mom sighed. "Well, I almost wish I was a member of Sarabiskota this summer. It's never boring being around you kids."

Kari smiled. "We'll make all you parents honorary members," she said.

"Yeah," said Jessie, "we're going to make new Sarabiskota T-shirts this summer, and we'll get one printed for each of you."

"That would be really nice," Mrs. Renner said.

That night, the nine teens did one of their favorite activities: they walked the full six miles up and down

Siesta Key Beach with flashlights. It couldn't have been a more beautiful night. The moon seemed unusually large and bright. Millions of stars lit up the summer sky above the limitless dark waters of the Gulf of Mexico.

As they walked along the beach barefoot, Kari whirled her flashlight around, shining it in the faces of her friends. "Hey, everyone. What time do you want me to get you up tomorrow morning for our exercise before breakfast?"

"What type of exercise do you have in mind?" Doc asked.

"How about a bike ride on the beach before sunrise?" Kevin suggested.

KT said, "The bikes are all ready to go at my house."

Kari said, "I could start waking everyone up at six. We could be out on the beach by six-thirty. That would give us an hour of exercise before breakfast."

"Sounds good to me," said Chad. "You can call my cell number and I'll wake up all the boys."

"I can't wait to start on our summer project," Jessie said excitedly.

"Me, too," said Doc. "Prez, do you really think

we can get it all done by August?"

"With all of us working together, I have no doubts," Prez said confidently.

Kari made sure everyone got up early the next morning. After a brisk bike ride up and down Siesta Key Beach, they ate breakfast, showered, and gathered outside KT's house.

From there, they rode their bicycles south approximately three miles on a road that ran parallel to the beach. They stopped when they got to a large, gold, rectangular, metal building. The building was easily big enough to hold a tennis court, and it had a huge Pittsburgh Steelers logo painted above the two large front doors.

They parked their bikes in front of the building, then followed Prez toward the doors. As they approached them, Prez said, "Open, sez me."

The metal doors slid open. As the nine teens entered, a polite female adult voice said, "Good morning, Prez. You're looking mighty handsome this fine morning. Good morning, KT, Doc, Kari, Jessie, Chad, Kevin, Mike, and Nick."

Everyone looked at Prez and laughed.

"What?" Prez said, trying his best not to laugh. "My computers like me."

As they walked farther into the building, several overhead lights automatically turned on and the full magnificence of Prez's workshop was on display. "Wow! This is so awesome!" Nick exclaimed.

"It's organized, too," Kari noted. "It's not like you, Prez."

"KT and Chad had a lot to do with that," Prez explained. "They helped me organize things in here the past month."

"It was a nightmare," Chad whispered loudly.

The nine teens slowly walked around the entire place as Prez explained some of his favorite projects.

"Thomas Edison would be proud of all this," said Kevin.

"I only wonder how much Edison could have done with all of this advanced stuff," Mike added.

That was definitely true. Prez's lab and workshop were stocked with the latest high tech computers and equipment. All around were various projects and inventions at different stages of completion.

"Come over here," Prez said. "I want to show you something."

Prez walked toward a large structure, cigar-shaped, about the size of a sofa. It resembled some type of engine.

"What is it?" Doc asked.

"It's a propulsion system I've been working on for quite a while," Prez answered. "It combines fuel cell, plasma magnet, and solar technologies. It might be just what we need for our project."

"Speaking of that," said Kari. "How do you suggest we get started this morning, Prez?"

"Let's head over to the Steelers Lounge area and talk about that right now," Prez replied.

Sarabiskota walked over to the other end of the building. There was a ping pong table, a pool table, a big screen television, two couches, and several other chairs. Almost everything was black and gold and had the Pittsburgh Steelers logo on it somewhere.

"Everyone relax," said Prez. "Here's how I suggest we get started ..."

The next two months flew by for Sarabiskota. The nine precocious teens were extremely busy, but they were also having the time of their lives. Working on a huge project with your best friends in one of the most beautiful places in the world was as good as it

could get.

But it wasn't all work and no play for Sarabiskota. They found time for long bike rides, boat rides, lots of beach time on Siesta Key, even some time to go to Busch Gardens and the Lowry Park Zoo in Tampa.

No matter what they were doing, though, their huge project was always on their minds. Could they possibly get it all done before some of them had to head back to Bismarck?

As the project went from planning stage to construction phase, the pace picked up and the activity around Prez's workshop became more intense. Numerous trucks arrived and delivered supplies.

Prez was surprised that none of his suppliers would charge him for anything he ordered. They had all heard of Prez and his friends before because of the famous treasure chest incident a year earlier. The suppliers all seemed honored to be part of whatever the nine precocious teens were working on this time.

Sarabiskota kept that a secret, though. Not even their parents knew what they were working on.

By the last day of July, the project was almost ready for testing outside the lab. In Prez's workshop,

Kevin and Prez were testing a few computer functions, while Jessie stood with a small paint brush in her right hand. She applied a few last strokes of orange paint to the object in front of her.

"I think that's it!" Jessie announced proudly.

Kevin and Prez joined the rest of Sarabiskota who stood back and admired their finished work.

"What a fantastic job!" KT said with pride.

"It's unbelievable!" Nick exclaimed.

"You guys all did great!" Prez said. "Now, I just hope it works as well outside the workshop as it did in the computer simulations inside."

Kevin giggled. "Thomas Edison would be proud of us."

"I wonder what Dr. Phil would think," Doc asked, trying to sound serious.

"What were you thinking?" Mike said, doing his best impression of Dr. Phil.

"I'm thinking we're ready for our first test flight tomorrow morning," said Prez. "We'll invite our parents, and we can send live video and audio feed to the parents back in North Dakota. They can watch it on their computers."

"Are you going to call any news media or anything?" Kari inquired.

"No," Prez replied. "They're probably going to find out about this soon enough."

That evening, the nine excited teens went for a long boat ride. After that, they watched a movie and went to bed.

The boys lay in their beds in the dark with only the faint glow of Nick's night light in the corner of the room.

Kevin said, "I wonder how this compares with the way the football players feel the night before the Super Bowl. It's hard to imagine being more pumped up than I am right now."

"No doubt," said Nick. "Although I'd rather compare it to the night before I drive in my first Daytona 500. How exciting would that be?"

Prez said, "All I know is, everyone's done such a great job on this project—except Chad, of course," he added jokingly.

"Prez, are you nervous at all?" Mike wanted to know.

"No doubt," Prez replied. "But it's a good kind of nervousness."

"I wonder if the girls are getting any sleep," said Chad. "If not, what do you think they're talking about right now?"

Nick giggled. "I can pretty much guarantee they're not talking about the Super Bowl or the Daytona 500."

"I'll bet they're talking about boys or shopping," Kevin guessed.

"There's only one way to find out," said Mike. "I'll call Kari."

Mike dialed Kari's cell phone number and she answered her phone on the first ring.

"Hi Kari. It's Mike. Are you girls getting any sleep?"

"Only Jessie. She can sleep through *anything*. The rest of us are talking and watching the movie *Where the Red Fern Grows*. How about you guys?"

"Not any sleep going on here, Kari. Too excited."

"Do you guys feel confident about everything?"

"Yup. Uh ... we've got a little bet going here. May I ask you what you girls were talking about when I called?"

"Yes, you may ask, but no, I'm not going to tell you. Just kidding. Actually, we were just debating who should have won *American Idol* this year. Doc admitted she liked the cute guy with the purple Mohawk hairstyle."

"That surprises me," Mike said, laughing. "I would've thought she liked the bald guy with the mustache."

"Mike, do you guys want to go for a walk on the beach tomorrow morning before we go to Prez's workshop?"

"Sure. What time?"

"Maybe seven?"

"Sounds good. I'll tell everyone else."

There were only three minutes left on the large digital countdown clock on the wall in Prez's workshop. Prez was running down the final checklist as his eight friends worked at their stations.

Prez called out, "All computer systems OK?"

"Computer systems are go," Kevin replied, looking at his computer monitor.

"Propulsion systems?" Prez asked.

"Propulsion systems are all ready," replied KT.

"Is the *Rough Rider* out in the bay and ready for filming?"

"Yes, Prez," Chad's dad responded from out

on the boat. "We can't wait to see what you've been working on."

"Mike, are you in position on the roof for filming?"

"I'm up here and ready," Mike announced.

Prez looked at one of the eight large TV monitors on the wall. He could see Mike standing on the huge Super Bowl XL logo painted on the roof of the workshop. Mike was holding the camera, ready to film.

"Nick, are you ready to send video to all the parents in Bismarck?"

"I'm ready, Prez."

"Bismarck, can you hear me now?"

"We hear you loud and clear," Jessie's mom replied from her home in Bismarck. All the parents from Bismarck were gathered at the Angel house and were watching and listening with great anticipation.

"Bismarck, are you receiving the video feeds?"

"Yes, we are. Good luck everyone down there in Sarasota!"

"Thank you. Doc, you may begin opening up the roof."

"Will do," said Doc.

Doc pushed a red button on the wall, and the

domed part of the roof slowly opened above them.

"All systems seem to be go as we approach the final countdown!" Prez said excitedly.

The countdown came down to the final ten seconds. "10... 9... 8... 7... 6... 5... 4... **3... 2... 1!"**

"Lift off!"

Suddenly, a beautiful, wonderful, unusual craft rose into the air from within Prez's workshop. It hovered briefly in the opening in the roof, then exited the building near the spot where Mike was standing. The craft rose another 50 feet straight into the air above the building and hovered there for several seconds.

Mike stood on the roof pointing the camera up in the air at the fantastic flying craft. The parents out on the *Rough Rider* and the parents in Bismarck watched in disbelief! Prez's dad was so surprised he almost dropped his camera into the Gulf of Mexico.

Several people walking the beach on this Saturday morning looked up at the flying thing and their jaws dropped. A little girl who was being pushed in a stroller pointed up into the sky and yelled, "Mommy, it's a flying *alligator!*"

"Oh, my! You're right honey!" her mom exclaimed. "It's a huge flying alligator!"

The little girl continued pointing and talking excitedly. "It's blue and orange and green and white. It's a pretty *alligator.* It's a really pretty *alligator!*"

The little girl's mother was speechless as she stared at the 40 foot alligator in the sky in front of her.

Prez gave a simple voice command into the microphone on his headset. "All right, *Gator Mikey.* Let's fly flight plan number 58."

At this point, the flying alligator rose to an altitude of 150 feet. As it was doing this, its big eyes were blinking and its enormous tail was moving from side to side. The next instant, Gator Mikey turned and started flying out over the water toward the *Rough Rider.*

Gator Mikey flew quietly and gracefully over the *Rough Rider.* Then he turned toward the north, flying at a slow speed parallel to the beach, approximately half a mile offshore.

"Dad, this is Prez. Please follow Gator Mikey and continue filming."

"Will do. Uh ... Son?"

"Yes, Dad."

"You kids have outdone yourselves. I never would have guessed your surprise would be a

gigantic flying alligator named Gator Mikey!"

"Thanks, Dad. You'll never believe what else Gator Mikey can do."

As Gator Mikey continued flying north, with the *Rough Rider* in close pursuit, Prez said, "All right. Let's test some of Gator Mikey's capabilities. KT, turn on Gator Mikey's cameras."

KT hit a few keys on her computer keyboard and suddenly two TV monitors on the wall showed the view from Gator Mikey's eyes.

Prez said, "Let's rotate the left eye camera so it's pointing toward the ground more ... Good ... Now the right camera."

"How's that?" KT asked.

"Great, KT. Now let's test the sound system on board Gator Mikey. Testing ... one, two, three. Dad, can you and the other parents hear me clearly on the boat?"

"Loud and clear."

"All right," said Prez. "Now, let's see if Gator Mikey can do what we really built him for."

Prez typed on his keyboard and Gator Mikey dropped down to an altitude below 100 feet. He flew closer to the beach where many people were now standing and watching in complete amazement.

"Hi, I'm Gator Mikey!" the flying gator spoke for the first time. His voice sounded just like the President of the United States! "I'm here to promote the learning of history and geography in Florida. **Are you smarter than a flying gator?** Try to answer my question if you can. I'll make it multiple choice so anyone can make a guess.

"What large body of water am I flying over right now? Is it A, the Gulf of Mexico; B, the Atlantic Ocean; or C, the Missouri River? I'll repeat the question and then give you ten seconds to think about it."

Gator Mikey repeated the question and then played soothing music for ten seconds. After that, he said, "I hope you made your guess and you get it right. The correct answer is A, the Gulf of Mexico. If you got it right, at the count of three, you can yell **I'm smarter than a flying gator!** 1 ... 2 ... **3!**"

"I'm smarter than a flying gator!" yelled most of the people down on the beach.

"That was great! If you got it wrong, don't worry. I have another question for you now. It's a much harder one, though. Here it is: Siesta Key Beach has some of the softest, whitest sand in the world. The sand never gets hot, no matter how hot and sunny the weather is. What substance in the sand makes this possible? Is it A, uranium; B, quartz; or C, thermos?

"Once again, I'll repeat the question and give you ten seconds to respond."

Gator Mikey repeated the question, then played some more soothing music for ten seconds.

"The correct answer is B, quartz. The sand is made of mostly quartz which reflects the heat. I hope you got it right. If you did, you know what to do at the count of three! 1 ... 2 ... **3!**"

"I'm smarter than a flying gator!" about half of the people yelled.

"If you didn't get it right, don't worry," Gator Mikey said, sounding just like the President of the United States. "I'll be asking many more history and geography questions in the future."

Prez said, "Good job, Gator Mikey. Time to return to the workshop. Let's try out your singing ability on the way back."

Gator Mikey had been programmed with many songs, many of them Elvis Presley songs. The flying gator's theme song was a special version of the famous Elvis song, "Hound Dog."

As Gator Mikey flew back toward the workshop, he sang his theme song enthusiastically:

I'm nothin' but a gator,
    Flyin' all the time,

I'm nothin' but a gator
    Flyin' all the time,

I'm promoting history and geography,
    And you can all be friends of mine!

As Gator Mikey was singing, the most incredible thing happened. Maybe it was the song; maybe it was the singing voice; maybe it was a combination of the two. Suddenly, thousands and thousands of love bugs began flying toward Gator Mikey from all directions. As the people on the ground watched in complete shock, swarms of love bugs landed on every square inch of Gator Mikey, totally covering him in no time at all.

"Oh, **NO!**"

"They're going to hurt Gator Mikey!"

"The love bugs are smothering Gator Mikey!"

"Can't we help him?"

"What can we do?"

Before anyone could utter another word, a huge **ZAP** of electricity flashed all around Gator Mikey.

Immediately, the entire massive mound of love bugs fell to the water like some strange black snow falling from the sky.

The next moment Gator Mikey turned and began flying north—away from Siesta Key—away from Prez's workshop!

6

"This is Heidi Godman from ABC-7 News in Sarasota. We're interrupting our regularly scheduled program to bring you this breaking news. For the past hour, I've been here with our news crew filming the sailboat races out on Sarasota Bay. Five minutes ago, we witnessed a most incredible sight. A huge blue, orange, and green alligator flew over Sarasota Bay directly toward us. After that, it flew right over us, then over that bank building there.

"Our cameraman, Hines Ward, was able to capture the whole thing on film. We'll show that unbelievable footage to you right now.

"You're getting a look at the alligator spaceship as it flew toward us. Incredibly, it made almost no sounds that you might expect from a flying aircraft like that.

"As you can see, the gator's jaws were opening and closing as it was flying, and its tail was moving back and forth. I'm estimating the gator flew over us at a speed of 60 miles per hour. It eventually flew over that bank building before it flew out of sight, apparently headed in the direction of Tampa Bay.

"The unusual sight got quite a reaction from the thousands of people here watching the sailboat races, but at this time we have no idea who the gator belongs to or where it's going. I can promise you ABC-7 News will look into it and keep you informed as more information comes in to us. For now, this is Heidi Godman reporting live from down at the Bayfront in Sarasota."

Within 20 minutes, all four major television stations in the Tampa-St. Petersburg area got word from the people at ABC-7 that a flying gator was headed their way. Until the Tampa newspeople saw the actual footage from Sarasota, however, they thought someone was playing a practical joke on them.

The TV stations' helicopters were in the air almost immediately. Less than fifteen minutes later, the Sky Fox 13 pilot was first to spot the gator aircraft approaching from the south.

Pilot Randy Powers described what he saw. "I thought I'd seen just about everything here in Florida, but this just might beat them all! We've got a gator traveling at a speed just under 100 miles per hour now headed north northeast. Our friends at ABC-7 in Sarasota first reported seeing this thing less than 30 minutes ago and, frankly, we thought they were joking. At this point we have no other information. We see no company logo anywhere on the gator. It's impossible to ignore the blue and orange colors on the aircraft, though. Is it possible the University of Florida has something to do with this? I don't have to remind anyone around here that blue and orange are the school colors of that university and the gator is the school mascot. I know they have an engineering department up there in Gainesville, but I don't think they design aircraft."

Governor Charlie Trust was swimming laps in his pool in Tallahassee, Florida, when he got a phone call from his chief of staff. He got out of the pool and answered the phone.

"Yes, George?"

"Governor, I thought you should know. We've got a big gator flying north over Tampa right now at an altitude of about 200 feet and a speed of approximately 100 miles per hour."

"You're joking, right?"

"No, it's on just about every TV network in America."

"Call Homeland Security, the National Guard, and the FAA immediately. I want a briefing in my office in 20 minutes."

The President of the United States was enjoying a relaxing day of fishing near Estes Park, Colorado. One of his Secret Service agents took a call. He walked out into the stream where the President was fishing.

"Mr. President, we have a situation. There's a flying alligator spaceship thing that just flew near McDill Air Force Base in Tampa. No one seems to know anything about the aircraft."

"You're serious?"

"Very serious, Sir. It's apparently on every television network."

"Why does so much of the really weird stuff seem to happen in Florida?"

"Uh ... I'm not sure, Mr. President. Anyway, that's not all, Sir. There have been some preliminary reports out of Sarasota that the flying alligator talks ... and it sounds just like *you*."

"Like *me*?"

"Yes, like you ... uh ... there's one more thing you should know."

"You mean there's more?"

"Yes, Mr. President. Apparently the gator sings like Elvis."

"Get the Vice President on the line—and see if we can get a TV out here. This is something I've got to see."

By this time, Prez's dad had contacted some of his friends in the government to explain the situation. In the meantime, Prez called Heidi Godman at ABC-7 to hopefully get the true story out to the news media.

Towards the end of the interview, Heidi asked, "Prez, what exactly do you think attracted all those love bugs to Gator Mikey?"

"I'm guessing it was the frequency of the sound he was emitting while singing the song."

"It was an Elvis song, right?"

"Yes, the song was essentially 'Hound Dog' with different lyrics."

"As I understand it, Gator Mikey emitted a huge bolt of electricity that killed all the bugs, but it also destroyed something else."

"That's right, Heidi. As far as we can tell, we no longer have control of where Gator Mikey goes. All of his other functions seem to be working just fine."

"What are you and your Sarabiskota friends doing right now?"

"We're all trying to fix the control problem. We're also following everything on television and watching the great video coming from the two cameras on Gator Mikey's eyes."

"You're getting video from cameras on Gator Mikey's eyes?"

"Yes, we can control where those cameras point and they have powerful zoom lenses, so we can get some fantastic views."

"Is there any way you can transfer that video link to us and we can share it with the other TV stations who want it?"

"Sure. When we're done with this interview, you can connect me to one of the engineers at your station ..."

By 12:45 p.m., Gator Mikey was approaching Gainesville. By this time, eight helicopters were following Gator Mikey. Two F-16's could also be seen in the sky.

The University of Florida football team had just returned to campus. They were having a light scrimmage at The Swamp, the name given to their football stadium.

Gator Mikey suddenly dropped down to a low altitude and approached the football stadium followed by the eight helicopters. The coaches and football players looked up in the air and stared at the unbelievable sight.

"What the heck?" Head Coach Suburban Meyer uttered as he gazed up at the flying gator. A few seconds later, the coach dropped his clipboard when Gator Mikey started to speak in the President's voice as he circled the stadium.

"Gainesville! It's great to be in **Gainesville!** Hi, I'm Gator Mikey! I'm here to promote the learning of history and geography in Florida. Try to answer this question if you can. I'll make it a multiple choice question to make it easier for you football players. Just kidding! You probably all know the answer to this question. Here goes!

"Gatorade was invented right here at the University of Florida by four researchers. Which NFL coach was the first to get a Gatorade dousing? Was it A, Bill Parcells; B, Don Shula; or C, Mike

Holmgren? I'll repeat the question and give you ten seconds to try to pick the correct answer."

Gator Mikey repeated the question. Then he sang some of the University of Florida's school song for ten seconds.

"OK. Time is up. I hope you picked the correct answer. It's A, Bill Parcells of the New York Giants. He got doused in 1985 by his defensive lineman, Jim Burt, after a win over the Washington Redskins.

"If you got the question correct, at the count of three, I want you to yell **I'm smarter than a flying gator!** 1 ... 2 ... **3!**"

"I'm smarter than a flying gator!" approximately one third of the football players and coaches yelled.

"Way to go! Now, I must be on my way! Guess where I'm going next? I'll give you a hint: **Gator Mikey's Back Street!**"

Gator Mikey circled the stadium one more time, then gained altitude and started flying south as he sang the University of Florida school song in his Elvis voice:

On, brave old Flor-i-da,
    Just keep on marching your way!

On, brave old Flor-i-da,
    And we will cheer you on your play!
Rah! Rah! Rah! ...

"This is Sue Triska from NBC News in New York. It appears the whole world has now turned its attention to Florida and Gator Mikey. Right now you're looking at Gator Mikey flying over The Villages area in Central Florida. This live action is being captured by the crew on board the NBC News 8 helicopter from Tampa, one of the many helicopters and other aircraft following Gator Mikey at this time. The fabulous flying gator is currently flying in a south southeasterly direction at approximately 125 miles per hour at an altitude of 350 feet.

"And what exactly do we know about this Gator Mikey so far? We know he speaks in the President's voice, sings like Elvis, and asks multiple choice questions having to do with history and geography.

"We know Gator Mikey was the creation of some extremely smart teens from Sarasota and North Dakota who call themselves Sarabiskota. You might have heard of them before. They were the same teens who found that treasure worth millions of dollars last year while looking for a lost sea captain.

"We also know Gator Mikey was supposed to be Sarabiskota's answer to Governor Charlie Trust's challenge to Florida teachers and kids. The last week of school, the governor challenged them to come up with projects to promote the learning of history and geography in the state.

"At ten o'clock this morning, just a little more than three hours ago, Sarabiskota was testing Gator Mikey near Siesta Key when a massive cloud of love bugs was somehow attracted to the flying gator while he was singing. Gator Mikey then emitted a huge charge of electricity that killed all the bugs, but may have sizzled some of the gator's circuits. Apparently, Sarabiskota has had no control over where Gator Mikey flies and what he says since then, although all other functions seem to be working fine.

"Where is the flying gator headed next? That seems to be totally up to Gator Mikey himself. He's given us this clue to his next destination: Gator Mikey's Back Street. This is Sue Triska reporting live from New York."

"Hi, Prez. This is Governor Trust."

"Hi, Governor. I'm sorry for all the trouble I'm

causing."

"Don't worry about it, Prez. Actually this might be turning out to be the greatest thing to happen to Florida since Walt Disney World. Right now almost everyone in the world is watching what your Gator Mikey is doing. Heck, the President is even watching."

"Really?"

"You bet. He's in Colorado on vacation keeping track as closely as everyone else. I think it's great when people all over the world are paying attention to our state for something other than hurricanes. The publicity is priceless for our state, Prez. Priceless!"

"I'm glad you think so, Governor."

"Well, I do. Anyway, I was calling to ask you if you might have any idea where Gator Mikey might be headed?"

"We think we know his next destination based on his clue, but after that—"

"You figured out his clue already?"

"I think so."

"Don't tell me the answer. I want to figure it out myself. Uh, I have another question for you, Prez."

"Sure, Governor."

"How long can Gator Mikey stay in the air before

he runs out of fuel?"

"A month or so assuming no other problems develop."

"A month without refueling? That's incredible! We've got to get together and talk about this sometime soon."

"I'd be happy to."

"Prez, do you foresee any problems or danger to anyone? If Gator Mikey collided with something or crashed to the ground, it wouldn't be good at all."

"Governor, Gator Mikey is built with advanced collision avoidance systems and they all seem to be fully operational."

"Great. I know you've seen the F-16's monitoring the situation at all times. They're instructed to shoot Gator Mikey down only if some danger seems imminent."

"Thank you, Governor."

"Thank *you*, Prez. What are you and your friends planning on doing now?"

"We're going to continue monitoring the situation from here and see if there's some way to regain control of Gator Mikey."

"Please keep me updated. Uh ... before we get off the phone, maybe you can give me one more little hint where you think Gator Mikey might be flying next ..."

People everywhere were following the progress of Gator Mikey. He seemed to be basically taking the path of U.S. Highway 27 in a south south easterly direction.

In Fort Collins, Colorado, four-year-old Laura Freese was looking at a map of Florida on the family's computer, trying to figure out where the flying gator was going next. Suddenly, she jumped up in the air and yelled, "I know where it's going to go next!"

"Where, Honey?" her mom asked.

"I'm not telling!" she replied.

Gator Mikey flew over the Citrus Tower, then over Haines City and the Bok Tower. Minutes later he flew over the Sebring International Raceway.

At this point, Gator Mikey began dropping in altitude as he approached Gatorama, one of Florida's oldest alligator attractions and an actual alligator farm. Millions of people watching around the world thought this would be the flying gator's next destination, but it was not to be.

As Gator Mikey flew over Gatorama, hundreds

of tourists waved and cheered. The crocodiles, alligators, monkeys, peacocks, and many other animals in the park created a huge ruckus.

Gator Mikey continued on, flying over the beautiful terrain of the Everglades. As he approached the intersection of County Road 833 and Interstate 75, he dropped down to an altitude of less than 100 feet. Then he turned west and flew directly over the interstate highway at a slow speed.

"Alligator Alley! It's great to be at **Alligator Alley!** Hi, I'm Gator Mikey! Did you guess my next stop would be Alligator Alley? That's the name for the 84 mile stretch of the toll way that runs across Big Cypress Swamp and the Everglades. A toll way is a road that you have to pay to drive on. Anyway, Alligator Alley got its name because many people thought building the road wasn't a good idea and only alligators would ever use it. Are you ready for my next question? Here it is: What was the official name given to this road when it first opened? Was it A, Panther Parkway; B, Seminole Highway; or C, Everglades Parkway?

"Once again, I'll repeat the question and give you ten seconds to think about your answer."

Gator Mikey repeated the question and hummed

a little of Elvis' song "Always on My Mind." After ten seconds he stopped singing and said, "The correct answer is C, Everglades Parkway, but Alligator Alley has now become the official name. If you got it right, you know what you can yell at the count of three. 1 ... 2 ... **3!**"

"I'm smarter than a flying gator!" millions of people all over the world yelled.

"That was great!" Gator Mikey exclaimed. "Well, I'll see you later. Where do you think I'm going next? I'll give you a little hint: **Tastes great with sausage!"**

"Hello, Governor Trust. This is the President again."

"Hi, Mr. President."

"What's the status there in Florida?"

"Well, Prez and his Sarabiskota friends are monitoring the entire situation. As of now, they have not regained control of Gator Mikey."

"Governor, I'm actually hoping this lasts longer. Our whole country is focused on something that's fun for a change. When's the last time that happened?"

"My feelings exactly, Mr. President. I shared them with Prez when I talked to him earlier."

"Where do you think Gator Mikey is headed next, Governor?"

"I'm not sure. He seems to be following an alligator theme: The Swamp in Gainesville which is the home of the Gators, then Alligator Alley."

"Oh ... that's right. I'm a little puzzled with this sausage clue, though."

"Me, too."

"Well, please continue to keep me informed."

"Will do, Mr. President. Good-bye."

"Good-bye."

Gator Mikey continued flying westward over Alligator Alley at a low altitude and a slow speed. On the highway below him, hundreds of motorists pulled their cars over to the side of the road and took pictures of the flying gator. The people cheered and yelled as Gator Mikey flew over them.

Shortly after he flew over the intersection of State Highway 29, Gator Mikey turned northwest, gained altitude, and accelerated to a speed of more than 325 miles per hour. The helicopters couldn't keep up with Gator Mikey any longer.

Fortunately, Gator Mikey's eye cameras were both working great. Anyone watching television or using their computer could get an excellent flying gator's eye view of the beautiful Florida landscape.

Back at Prez's workshop on Siesta Key, Sarabiskota was monitoring everything closely.

Kevin reported, "Gator Mikey just flew over a town named Corkscrew. If he stays on this course, it looks like Lehigh Acres is next."

"How did the town Corkscrew get its name?" asked Nick.

"I'm reading about that right now," said Doc. "There's a swamp nearby that's shaped like a corkscrew. They named the town after the swamp."

"What's the population?" Jessie inquired.

"It must be really small," KT noted. "No population is even listed."

"Hey Prez," said Kari. "With his present course and speed, Gator Mikey will be over the Gulf of Mexico in less than 30 minutes."

"Thanks, Kari," Prez replied. "I think I have a good idea where he's going. I'm also noting a little pattern developing in the towns he's choosing."

"Where's he going next and what pattern are you talking about?" Nick asked eagerly.

"Are you sure you want me to tell you, Nick?" Prez asked. "It's much more fun when you figure it out yourself."

"You're right," said Nick. "Don't tell me ... *yet.*"

Sarabiskota followed Gator Mikey's nearly straight-lined course over Port Charlotte, a ghost town named Verna, and the town of Parrish.

As he was flying over Tampa Bay, Chad pointed at the screen of one of the televisions on the wall and yelled, "Hey, look! They're even covering Gator Mikey on the Weather Channel."

"Turn up the volume on that TV and mute the others," KT requested.

Tommy Tornado, one of the Weather Channel forecasters, was speaking: "We're right in the middle of hurricane season here in Florida; however, there are no hurricanes developing at this time. But people are following Gator Mikey with more intensity and interest than any hurricane. Instead of them rushing to get out of the way of an approaching hurricane, people are doing everything they can to get into Gator Mikey's path so they can be part of history in Florida. We have a correspondent, Tammy Typhoon, who's in Dunedin, Florida, right now with more on this story."

"That's exactly right, Tommy. Right now, I'm in Dunedin, Florida, where hundreds of people are gathered here on Main Street. With any luck, Gator Mikey should fly over us shortly if he continues on his present course. Standing on my right is the mayor of Dunedin, Bob Hackworth. Mayor, tell us a little about your beautiful community."

"Thanks, Tammy. I'm a big fan of yours. Let me first say how excited I am to be here with all these great people!" The crowd cheered and some waved signs in the air.

The mayor continued speaking, "I think Gator Mikey would be especially proud of Dunedin, Tammy. Not many people know this, but the *Alligator* has actually played an important part in Dunedin's history and the history of our country as well."

"What do you mean, Mayor?" Tammy Typhoon asked.

"Well, back during World War II, the people from this town actually assembled a rather strange looking amphibious tractor called the Alligator. It moved troops and supplies around and played a big part in our side winning the war."

"Cool, Mayor," said Tammy Typhoon. "Do you happen to know how your town got its name?"

"I sure do. We were called Jonesboro in the 1870's because the guy that owned the general store was named George Jones. Then two Scottish merchants named the post office and town Dunedin in 1882. Dunedin is the old Gaelic name for Edinburgh, Scotland, and our city had many settlers from that country."

"What's *Gaelic?*" Tammy Typhoon wanted to know.

"All I know, it's an old language once spoken in Scotland."

"Oh. What are some of the things Dunedin is known for?"

"Well, we once were an important seaport and trading center. In fact, we had the largest fleet of sailing ships in Florida at one time. We were the first home of the PGA, the Professional Golfers Association. Besides that, we were the first town *ever* to make orange juice concentrate."

"That's very interesting—oh, my! Here comes Gator Mikey!"

The whole crowd's attention turned toward the sky as Gator Mikey approached from the southeast. He slowed down to almost a crawl and swooped down over the crowd on Main Street. Then he flew out over the Gulf of Mexico heading northwest.

"I think I heard Gator Mikey singing 'Tutti Fruitti' as he flew over us!" Tammy Typhoon exclaimed. "That's one of my mom's favorite Elvis songs."

By this time, *almost* everyone in the world knew about Gator Mikey. Not the six men on board the fishing trawler *Sea Sick,* though. They'd been fishing out on the Gulf of Mexico for the last five days and hadn't heard any news at all during that time.

As the men busied themselves on board, Captain Jack Collins thought he saw a strange looking aircraft off the bow. As it got closer, Captain Jack yelled to his men something he never dreamed he'd *ever* say, "Flying gator off the port bow!"

Gator Mikey hit land again near Bald Point State Park on Florida's panhandle. He flew over Highway 98 and then the Apalachicola National Forest. Shortly before 5:00 p.m., Gator Mikey slowed down, dropped down to an altitude of 100 feet, and began circling two small general stores built at a crossroads.

"Hi, I'm Gator Mikey! I'm promoting the learning of history and geography in Florida. **Two Egg!** This is **Two Egg,** Florida! What a great name for a little town! See if you can answer this question about how Two Egg got its name. Once again, I'll make it a multiple choice question so anyone can guess. Here goes: It's believed Two Egg got its name from whom? Was it A, two children; B, a traveling salesman; or C, Walt Disney?

"I'll repeat the question and give you ten seconds to think about your answer."

Gator Mikey repeated the question and hummed

the beginning of the song "America the Beautiful" for ten seconds.

"The correct answer is B, a traveling salesman. As the story goes, a traveling salesman who did business with the owner of the general store noticed kids coming in and trading one or two eggs for candy. He started calling the place Two Egg Town, but it eventually became just Two Egg.

"Now, if you got the question correct, you know what to yell at the count of three! Ready? 1 ... 2 ... **3!**"

"I'm smarter than a flying gator!" about 50 people on the ground in Two Egg and millions more around the world yelled.

"That was brilliant!" said Gator Mikey. "Now, guess where I'm going next? I'll give you a hint: **Big water!"**

Gator Mikey took off in a southeasterly direction at 200 miles per hour. Back at Prez's workshop, Sarabiskota charted the progress of Gator Mikey as he flew over St. Marks, then over the Gulf of Mexico, then over land again at Cedar Key.

"It's pretty obvious where he's going this time," said Chad.

"Yup," Kevin confirmed. "I just found out its name means *big water* in the Hitchiti Indian language."

"Huh?" Nick said. "You guys are way ahead of me."

"Prez, we're not too far from sunset," Kari noted. "Do you think Gator Mikey's going to fly all night?"

"No idea," said Prez. "If he decides to, he certainly has plenty of lights."

Jessie giggled. "That's an understatement."

Gator Mikey had made it to Lake Okeechobee by 7:00 p.m. As he flew low over the lake, the flying gator called out, **"Okeechobee!** Lake **Okeechobee** is the fourth largest natural lake that's completely within the United States. If you know any of the three natural lakes that are larger, you're way too smart! But that's not my question. The question is: Which President of the United States flew training missions over this huge lake as a pilot? Was it A, George Washington; B, George H.W. Bush, our 41st President; or C, George W. Bush, our 43rd President?"

Gator Mikey repeated the question and then hummed ten seconds of "Hail to the Chief," the official anthem of the President of the United States.

After that, he said, "This was a tough question since both of the presidents named Bush were pilots. The correct answer is B, George H. W. Bush, the 41st President. At age 18, he was the youngest Navy pilot in World War II, and he trained over this lake in the 1940's.

"If you got the answer correct, you know exactly what to say at the count of three. 1 ... 2 ... **3!**"

"I'm smarter than a flying gator!"

"Now, guess where I'm going next? I'll give you a hint: **It's John and Mable's place!"**

"Prez!" Chad exclaimed. "I think Gator Mikey's coming back to Sarasota!"

"I think you're right," Prez replied excitedly. "Let's hustle home and get on the *Rough Rider!*"

With less than half an hour remaining until sunset, Gator Mikey approached Sarasota from the East. Meanwhile, Sarabiskota raced north in Sarasota Bay in the *Rough Rider.*

"Kari, do you think Gator Mikey's returning home for good?" KT asked.

"I sure hope not," replied Kari. "This is too much fun."

"Wow!" Nick exclaimed. "Look at all the boats headed our way."

There were hundreds of boats around them, all going north, just like they were. Gator Mikey's clue referring to *John and Mable's place* was an easy one for Sarasota people to solve. Gator Mikey's next destination was pretty obvious. It was the Ringling Complex on Shell Beach. That's where John and Mable Ringling from the famous Ringling Circus family had built a world class art museum and a beautiful home called the Cà d'Zan.

By the time the Rough Rider got to Shell Beach, there were only about fifteen minutes until sunset. The United States Coast Guard was patrolling the water, now packed with hundreds of boats. Thousands of people waited on land near the Ringlings' house and art museum. The excitement and anticipation was unbelievable!

Finally, Gator Mikey came into view. He flew over the art museum, over the Ringlings' home, then out over all the boats floating on Sarasota Bay. At this point Gator Mikey started turning around over the water less than one hundred yards from where the *Rough Rider* was anchored. What he did next took everyone's breath away.

A loud **"Awwwwww!"** came from the crowd as Gator Mikey turned on all his lights. And what an impressive array of lights it was! Thousands of mostly orange, blue, and green lights lit up the entire night sky. There were spot lights, blinking lights, and pulsating lights. It was a light extravaganza!

Out on the *Rough Rider,* the nine teenagers cheered.

"Jessie, your ideas for the lights were obviously terrific," Chad said.

"Just incredible!" KT added.

"It's awesome!" Nick exclaimed.

Gator Mikey slowly flew back toward the Ringlings' home. When he got within 100 yards, he suddenly dropped down to an altitude a mere 50 yards above the treetops. Still flying at a slow speed, he began circling the art museum and the Ringling home.

"**Ringling!** This is the art museum and house that John and Mable **Ringling** built here in Sarasota. The Ringling Brothers and Barnum & Bailey Circus had their winter quarters in Sarasota from 1927 until 1960. This was really Circus Town USA. Here's my question for you. It's a colorful question, just like my lights.

"What color was considered bad luck to the Ringling circus performers? Was it A, blue; B, orange; or C, green?

"Once again, I'll repeat the question for you and blink all my lights for ten seconds before I give the correct answer."

After repeating the question and blinking his lights for ten seconds, Gator Mikey said, "OK. Time is up. The correct answer is C, green! At the count of three, I want *everyone* to say **Let's party all night! 1 ... 2 ... 3!**"

"Let's party all night!"

Gator Mikey started blinking all his lights and singing "Lucy in the Sky With Diamonds," only he changed the lyrics slightly:

Gator Mikey in the sky with diamonds!
Gator Mikey in the sky with diamonds!

As the whole huge crowd of people sang along, Gator Mikey turned and flew west, increasing his altitude to over 400 feet. After that, he began flying a circular, clockwise path over the entire Sarasota area.

It was spectacular! On this crystal clear night, Gator Mikey could be seen for miles. Billions watched on television throughout the world.

This whole Gator Mikey idea was supposed to be a way to promote geography and history in Florida, and it was definitely accomplishing that. Clearly, though, something even more important was happening. For at least this one day, the whole world had come together to share a common experience— a *fun* experience!

Sarabiskota watched from out on the bay before returning to Siesta Key in the dark. When they got back home, the whole island seemed to be having a party.

As they were getting the boat back on the trailer, Nick said, "Well, I always say it never gets boring around you guys—but this may be ridiculous."

"No doubt," said Doc. "I just wonder if Gator Mikey has even more in store for us."

"I sure hope so," said Kevin.

Prez's cell phone started to ring, so he answered it.

"Hello? This is Prez."

"Hi, Prez. This is Governor Trust."

"Oh, hi, Governor."

"Sounds like lots of commotion going on wherever you are. What are you doing?"

"We just got back from the Ringling Complex. Our whole neighborhood on Siesta Key seems to be having a Gator Mikey party. It's pretty amazing."

"Tallahassee is pretty wild, too. Prez, any guesses on what's going to happen next?"

"My friends and I were just talking about that. We're literally clueless. Gator Mikey gave us no clue to help us this time."

"Prez, if by some chance Gator Mikey leaves the Sarasota area, would you kids like to follow him? I can make arrangements for a small private jet to be waiting for you at the Sarasota-Bradenton International Airport just in case."

"That would be awesome!"

"Why don't you give me your dad's cell phone number and I'll make sure it's OK with all your parents."

"Sure, Governor Trust."

"Prez, whatever happens, I'd like to meet you and your friends sometime in the next few days."

"That would be great, Governor Trust ..."

Meanwhile, at the Stanley Hotel in Estes Park, Colorado, the President was up late watching what was transpiring with great interest. He picked up his phone and pushed one button.

"Governor Trust, this is the President."

"Hi, Mr. President."

"What a day you've had down there in Florida! I wish I could have witnessed it all in person. Look, the reason I'm calling ... I still have several days of vacation scheduled here. But if this Gator Mikey thing goes on, I sure would like to come to Florida and be part of it."

"We'd love to have you, Mr. President."

"Great! I'll talk to the Secret Service and everyone else to see if it's even feasible. I'd love to chase Gator Mikey in Air Force One for awhile. Maybe you and Sarabiskota could be my guests."

"I'd love to do that. I know the kids would be thrilled."

"Uh, one more thing, Governor."

"Yes, Mr. President."

"I've heard that many people have figured out some pattern for the five locations Gator Mikey flew over after he left Siesta Key. Do you know what it is?"

"I think so, Sir."

"Don't tell me the answer ... but maybe you can give me a little hint."

"All right. Let's see. Five locations, five letters, one reptile."

"Five locations, five letters, one reptile?"

"Yes."

"I've got it. I'll call you tomorrow. Good night, Governor."

"Good night, Mr. President."

10

As the sun rose at Siesta Key, the nine exhausted teens slept soundly in the two tents they'd pitched on the beach. After one of the most exciting, eventful days of their lives, they hadn't gotten to sleep until nearly three o'clock in the morning.

In the boys' tent, Kevin was brought out of a deep sleep by what he thought was the sound of music coming from a radio. He listened for awhile and recognized the song as one of his mom's favorites, a Beatles song, "Here Comes the Sun."

Kevin sang along in his head as the music became louder: *"Here comes the sun, nah nah nah nah ..."*

Suddenly, Kevin realized the familiar music was coming from the sky!

He sat up and whispered loudly, "Hey guys! Get up! Gator Mikey's flying right over us!"

Kevin was out of the tent in three seconds and his good friends weren't far behind.

As they looked up in the air, there was Gator

Mikey! He was hovering 20 yards above the surface of the water, just 30 yards away from where they were standing.

"I've got to get the girls up," Chad whispered slowly as he stared up at Gator Mikey who seemed to be staring right back at him.

Chad and Nick ran over to the girls' tent.

"I can tell there's some recognition on his part," Prez observed. "Some of those circuits must still be working."

"Should we talk to him or something?" Mike whispered.

The girls ran over and joined the boys. They gazed up at Gator Mikey, who seemed to recognize the nine teens, at some level at least.

"Yes, talk to him," Prez whispered. "Maybe he'll figure out who we are."

"Gator Mikey, it's me, Jessie. I helped design you and give you your lights and fabulous paint job."

"Gator Mikey, I'm Kevin. I helped program you with all the historical and geographical information. You've been using it to come up with your multiple choice questions."

"Hi, Gator Mikey. I'm Kari. I got things organized each day so we could finish building you quickly. Do you remember me?"

Gator Mikey seemed focused on what the teens were saying.

"I think he recognizes us," said Nick. "Let's keep talking."

"Gator Mikey, it's me, Mike. I programmed all those songs in your data banks. That's my voice you're using when you sing your songs."

Mike started singing "Here Comes the Sun" softly in his Elvis voice. "Here comes the sun, nah, nah, nah, nah ..."

This seemed to trigger something in Gator Mikey. He started singing again:

Here comes more fun,
　　Nah, nah, nah, nah,
Here comes more gator fun,
　　And I say,
It's time to go now,
　　Fun, fun, fun, here we come ...

Gator Mikey turned and took off at a slow speed, flying northwest toward Longboat Key. Kari looked at her friends. "Time to head for the airport!" she said anxiously.

Chad's mom and dad rushed the nine teens to the airport in the van. On the way, Sarabiskota could actually see Gator Mikey flying slowly in a northwesterly direction above the beaches on the Gulf of Mexico side of Longboat Key.

"Where do you guys think he's going?" Chad's dad asked.

Doc had her computer on her lap. "On his present course, he's headed straight for Tallahassee," she noted.

Nick giggled. "If he keeps traveling at this speed, we could almost catch him in a golf cart. He's barely moving."

"It's almost like he's waiting for us to catch up with him," said Jessie.

"No doubt," said Kevin. "Do you think he's playing a game with us?"

"I have no idea," Prez replied. "But it's as good an explanation as any."

"Mrs. Renner, thanks for volunteering to come with us today," said Kari.

"How could I possibly pass up an experience like this?" Mrs. Renner replied. "It will be my first experience on a private jet."

"Do all of you have everything you need?" Mr.

Renner asked.

"Doc and I double-checked everything before we loaded up," Kari answered.

Prez's cell phone rang.

"Hello?"

"Hi, Prez. This is Governor Trust. Are you at the airport yet?"

"Almost, Governor."

"Any ideas about Gator Mikey's next destination?"

"We could actually see him flying north off Longboat Key a few minutes ago. He's flying really slow. Doc says he's on course for Tallahassee right now, but that could change any time."

"Tallahassee would be great. That's where I am now and I have several meetings here today."

"On a Sunday, Sir?"

"Yes, even on Sunday. Well, you all have a good flight. I'll give you a call later."

"Thanks, Governor. Bye."

"Good-bye, Prez."

Gator Mikey flew over the southern half of Longboat Key, then he headed straight north. He flew right over a group of kids playing in front of Sea

Breeze Elementary School in Bradenton. After that, he flew over the DeSoto National Monument at the mouth of the Manatee River. The flying gator then turned sharply to the east and flew up the Manatee River all the way to the Bradenton City Pier.

There, he slowed down and started circling a large building nearby, where a huge crowd was already gathering.

"Manatee!" Gator Mikey boomed. "We're here at the Parker Manatee Aquarium in the city of Bradenton. Bradenton is the county seat of Manatee County. This is the home to the oldest manatee in captivity in the whole world, Snooty! He came to this aquarium from Miami in 1949 when he was just a baby. Hi, Snooty!"

Snooty looked up into the sky through the clear plastic domed aquarium. The huge flying gator above him was calling his name! Snooty used his front flippers and lifted himself right out of the water and squeaked with excitement.

"Here's my question for Snooty and all the rest of you. Besides Manatee County, how many of the 67 counties in Florida are named after animals? Is it A, zero; B, one; or C, two? Of course, I'll repeat the question and give you ten seconds to answer."

Gator Mikey repeated the question and sang ten seconds of the Elvis song "It's Now Or Never."

After that, he said, "The answer is A, zero. None of the other counties in Florida are named after animals besides Manatee County. There once was a Mosquito County in Florida, but who would want to live there? They changed the name to Orange County. Now, what do you yell if you got the question correct?"

"I'm smarter than a flying gator!"

"Fantastic! Well, good-bye Snooty! Good-bye everyone! Where do you think I'm flying to next? I'll give you a hint: **Ichepuckesassa! Ichepuckesassa! Ichepuckesassa!"**

Sarabiskota followed Gator Mikey's activity at the aquarium on their computers while they waited to board their jet.

"Ichepuckesassa! Ichepuckesassa!" Kevin repeated.

"It has such a nice rhythm to it," Jessie said as she started dancing around the airport terminal while chanting the strange sounding word. Soon, her eight friends joined in the little dance.

"Sounds more like a disease some hockey player might get," Nick said as he danced around. "Doc, do you have a prescription for Ichepuckesassa?"

"Not for that," Doc replied, giggling. "But you may need a prescription for that dancing of yours."

Everyone started laughing so much they couldn't dance any more.

"Has anyone found any information about Ichepuckesassa at all?" Kari asked.

"There's a creek up in Hillsborough County with a similar name," Prez replied, "but no towns I could find."

A lady and two men approached them and introduced themselves. First, there was Ron Ladd, a friendly, short man in his early thirties with a slight southern accent. He turned out to be the flight attendant.

"It's an honor to be on the same aircraft as the famous Sarabiskota," he said with a smile as he shook all their hands. "My daughter is in the third grade, and she's so jealous of me getting to fly with y'all."

The other two people introduced themselves as Jan Alcorn and Justin Fischer. Jan was a tall, pretty, brunette. She turned out to be a reporter from a television station in Montpelier, Vermont. It was easy to tell what Justin did. The young, athletic looking man was carrying a television camera.

Jan explained, "Justin and I were the lucky ones to have our names drawn out of a hat. It's our job to cover you and this big story while you're on board the jet and share the information with the rest of the news media around the world. If we get in your way too much, please let us know."

Finally, they boarded the aircraft, a beautiful Gulfstream III jet.

"Oh, my gosh!" Kari exclaimed when she first got on board.

"Look at all the room in here!" Kevin added.

"This is definitely going to be fun," said Jessie.

Ron said, "Make yourselves comfortable and buckle in. You can move around anywhere you'd like once we get in the air."

The pilot came over the intercom. "This is your pilot, Ward Larsen. We're about ready to take off on *Sarabiskota Airlines.* Our special mission is to follow Gator Mikey wherever he goes. My copilot, John Wanner, and I are happy to be part of this historic journey. If there's anything we can do to make your trip more enjoyable, please let us know."

At the same time they were taking off, Gator Mikey was flying over the Sunshine Skyway Bridge near St. Petersburg. After their jet had reached sufficient altitude, the nine teens gathered in the lounge area and turned on their computers to see what was happening.

"Gator Mikey has turned northeast and increased his speed," Chad reported.

"It looks like he'll fly right over downtown Tampa," Mike added.

"I think I know exactly where he's headed,"

Jessie said excitedly.

"Where?" asked Nick.

"Look," she said, pointing at her computer screen. "There's no town named Ichepuckesassa, but there used to be. That's where he's flying."

Sarabiskota's jet caught up with Gator Mikey as he approached Brandon, Florida. As large numbers of people watched and cheered from the ground below, Gator Mikey flew above Interstate 4 on the way to Plant City.

Gator Mikey approached the Main Street of Plant City at an altitude of just 50 feet. A huge crowd on the ground was chanting **"Ichepuckesassa! Ichepuckesassa! Ichepuckesassa!"**

Gator Mikey flew on a little farther until he got to Dinosaur World, a wooded park and picnic area filled with 150 life-size dinosaurs. He started circling the area as the people down below him cheered loudly.

Gator Mikey yelled, **"Ichepuckesassa!** This is Plant City now, but it used to be called **Ichepuckesassa.** Ichepuckesassa is a Creek Indian word meaning *tobacco field.* The word was so hard to spell and pronounce, the people here decided to change it to Cork. After that, it became Plant City, but it's not named after all the plants grown around here. It's named after a famous railroad tycoon named Henry Plant. Now, I've got a question that everyone from Plant City probably already knows the answer to, so please don't yell the answer until I ask you to later. The question is: What fruit is Plant City most famous for? Is it A, watermelons; B, tomatoes; or C, strawberries?

"Once again, I'll repeat the question and give you ten seconds to think about this, even though most of you already know the answer."

Gator Mikey repeated the question. Then he sang a little of the song "Whole Lotta Shakin' Goin' On" while dancing in the sky.

"All right! Time is up!" the flying gator yelled. "At the count of three, everyone can call out the answer at the same time. 1 ... 2 ... **3!**"

"Strawberries!"

"That's right," said Gator Mikey. "The correct answer is C, strawberries. Plant City is known as the winter strawberry capital of the world. Its strawberry festival in late February and early March is awesome! They once made the world's largest strawberry shortcake there. It weighed over 6,000 pounds and was a whopping 827 square feet!

"Let me know if you got the question correct—right **now!**"

"I'm smarter than a flying gator!"

"Now, where do you think I'm going next? I'll give you a hint: **Ham the Chimp.**"

"Mr. President. This is Governor Trust. We may have a problem."

"Go ahead, Governor."

"I just got a call from Prez. Gator Mikey seems to be flying east northeast out of Plant City at over 300 miles per hour. We think we know where he's going, and that's the problem."

"Where's he going?"

"Directly toward Kennedy Space Center—and I know unauthorized aircraft aren't allowed within that airspace."

"Give me a few minutes. I'll take care of it."

"Thank-you, Mr. President."

"You're welcome. By the way, Governor, what's the deal with Ham the Chimp?"

"That's an interesting story, Mr. President. It happened back in 1961 when I was just a kid, so I'd forgotten about it. It turns out Ham the Chimp was launched into space about three months before Alan Shepherd."

"Wasn't there a dog launched before the chimp?"

"Yes, the Russians did that. Her name was Laika. They sent her into space in 1957."

"Do you know what happened to Ham the Chimp?"

"Yup. I've been reading about that. He had a good life spent at the National Zoo and the North Carolina Zoo. Sounds like he made several TV appearances, even a film with daredevil Evil Knievel."

"What an interesting story! Well, I'd better take care of our little problem. I'll get back to you later today about my possible trip to Florida."

"Fantastic. Thanks, Mr. President."

"You're very welcome. Good-bye."

"Good-bye."

Gator Mikey approached Kennedy Space Center, escorted by four F-16's. Behind Gator Mikey, four Shuttle Training Aircraft, piloted by four astronauts, were flying in formation. They didn't want to miss out on the fun.

The Gulfstream III was flying behind the

astronauts. On board, Sarabiskota watched in wonder as they flew over the launch pads, the visitor complex, the shuttle landing facility, and all the other sites they'd all seen on television before.

Gator Mikey began circling the biggest building of them all. **"Kennedy Space Center!"** the flying gator called. "Kennedy Space Center is named after President John F. Kennedy, a huge supporter of the space program. The Vehicle Assembly Building down below is one of the largest buildings in the world. It has the largest doors in the whole wide world on it! The question is: How high are the doors? For your reference, the Statue of Liberty is 305 feet tall, and a football field from goal line to goal line is 300 feet. So, knowing that, do you think the doors on the Vehicle Assembly Building are: A, 310 feet high; B, 359 feet high; or C, 456 feet high?

"Of course, I'm going to repeat the question and give you ten seconds to think about your answer." Gator Mikey did repeat the question and then he sang the song "Rocket Man" for ten seconds.

"All right. Time is up. The answer is C, 456 feet high. The Vehicle Assembly Building is so big you could fit almost four Statues of Liberty inside. Is anyone smarter than a flying gator?"

"I'm smarter than a flying gator!"

"Wow! That was great! Now, I'll bet you have no idea where I'm going next. I'll give you a hint, but it's probably too tough for any of you: **a big, mean, red-eyed alligator monster!"**

Gator Mikey turned and began flying west northwest at almost 500 miles per hour.

On board the Gulfstream III, Sarabiskota and Chad's mom were having the time of their lives. Jan Alcorn was finishing an interview with Chad's mom.

"Mrs. Renner, how were you picked to accompany these nine bright teens today?"

"Actually, I volunteered quickly. How could I pass this up?"

"Are you enjoying yourself so far?"

"I feel like royalty. Ron has made sure I have anything I want."

"I should explain to our viewers that Ron is our flight attendant, Ron Ladd. He is truly great at his job. Now I'm going over to where the nine teens are doing their research. This is Kari Wise. Kari, what are you doing?"

"Could I just say hi to my family and everyone else in North Dakota first? Uh, we just got an e-mail from a man who lives up on the panhandle of Florida. He thinks he knows something about the monster alligator with the red eyes. I'm e-mailing him back to get more information."

"Thanks, Kari. Right next to Kari is Prez. Prez, I understand you've been communicating with Governor Charlie Trust of Florida."

"Yes, he called just a few minutes ago and he said he's going to try to join us tomorrow—if Gator Mikey keeps flying. He also mentioned he might be bringing a famous friend with him."

"I wonder who that could be."

"I have no idea."

"I can't wait to find out, and I'll bet our viewers are curious now too. For now, this is Jan Alcorn reporting from on board the Gulfstream III with Sarabiskota."

Gator Mikey slowly approached the town of Esto, Florida, at a low altitude. The whole population of 350 people was outside waiting for this, and thousands of other people had come from other places to share the experience.

Gator Mikey began circling the town at a slow speed. **"Esto!"** he yelled. **"Esto** is the home of the

Two-Toed Tom Festival! The festival is named after an infamous, red-eyed, monster gator who attacked people and animals around this area for years! People tried to hunt him down, trap him, or blow him up with dynamite, but nothing seemed to stop Two-Toed Tom! He got his name because he lost some of his toes on his left front foot in a bear trap. The question is: How many toes does an alligator usually have on his front foot? Is it A, five; B, four; or C, three?"

Gator Mikey repeated the question and made his eyes blink red for ten seconds.

"The answer is A, five," Gator Mikey announced. "An alligator has five toes on his front feet and four on his hind feet. Was anyone smarter than *me* on that question?"

"I'm smarter than a flying gator!"

"Now, I'm not going to tell you where I'm flying next. Why not? Why should I? Why, oh, why, oh, **why?"**

12

With slightly more than an hour left before sunset, Gator Mikey was circling Ybor City.

"Ybor City!" he called out. "Ybor City is now a part of Tampa, but it once had five times the population of Tampa. Ybor City is named after Vincente Martinez-Ybor who brought his factory to Tampa in 1886. Then he bought 40 acres of land that eventually became Ybor City. The question is: What did Ybor's factory and the other factories in Ybor City make by hand? Was it A, Barbie dolls; B, cigars; or C, computers?"

Gator Mikey repeated the question. After that, he released blue and orange smoke from his tail end for ten seconds. The huge crowd gathered below him laughed and cheered.

"OK. Time is up. The correct answer is B, cigars. Ybor City once had 200 cigar factories and made more than one million cigars a day. Now, what do you yell if you got the question right?"

"I'm smarter than a flying gator!"

"Excellent! You might have a better idea where I'm going for sunset when I start singing this Beach Boys song!"

Gator Mikey started singing the song "Kokomo," and soon, the whole crowd in Ybor City was singing along with the fantastic flying gator.

"Gator Mikey's headed for sunset off the Florida Keys!" Jessie exclaimed on board the Gulfstream III flying overhead. "It's in the song!"

"He's turning and flying southeast," Kevin noted. "I think you're right, Jessie."

Gator Mikey flew at a speed exceeding 400 miles per hour toward the Florida Keys, singing the same Beach Boys song as he flew.

On board their jet, Kevin was doing some calculating. "At this course and speed, we'll be in the keys in about half an hour."

Prez said, "I wonder what key he's going to choose to stop at."

"Just for the fun of it," Kari began, "I checked to see if there's an Alligator Key down there someplace. It turns out there's an Alligator Reef with a lighthouse on it. The reef was named after a schooner by the name of the *USS Alligator.* The *Alligator* wrecked on the reef in 1822."

"What's a schooner again?" asked Nick.

Doc answered, "It's a ship with at least two masts with fore and aft sails."

"Oh."

"What wrecked the *USS Alligator*?" Chad wanted to know.

"Well," said Kari, "it was chasing pirates and escorting ships when it ran aground on the reef. After some other ships rescued the crew and salvaged some of the ship, they actually set the ship on fire and blew it up."

"Why?" KT inquired.

"So the pirates wouldn't get anything good out of it," Kari answered. "Anyway, after that, the lighthouse was built on the reef so no other ships would run aground on it again."

"Cool," said Nick.

"How many islands are there in the Florida Keys?" asked Jessie.

"One source here says 700, another says 900," Prez replied. "Here's one that says 1,700."

"Can't they count things down here in Florida?" asked Nick.

Prez giggled. "There was that counting problem

in the election of 2000—but as far as the number of keys goes, I have a feeling they just can't agree on how big a land mass has to be before it's classified as an island. Some islands in the Florida Keys aren't much bigger than Gator Mikey."

Doc said, "It says here that the Florida Keys cover a distance of about 220 miles. There's a highway that connects many of the keys that's 127 miles long. They call it the Overseas Highway or U.S. Route 1."

"Wow!" said Mike. "They've even got a bridge on that highway between two of the keys called the Seven Mile Bridge, but it's *only* 6.8 miles long."

Everyone looked at Nick, expecting a comment or question. Nick giggled when he noticed everyone looking at him. "What?" he said. "I was just thinking 6.8 Mile Bridge isn't as cool a name as Seven Mile Bridge. Plus, they just rounded it to the nearest whole number."

Jan Alcorn and Justin Fischer came over to where Sarabiskota was working. Jan said, "There are several e-mails coming in from all over the country with questions. Would you mind answering some of them on camera?"

Kari spoke for the whole group. "Not at all," she said.

"All right," Jan said. "We'll begin in three seconds. 1 ... 2 ... 3! Hi, this is Jan Alcorn on board Gulfstream III with Sarabiskota. We think we're following Gator Mikey down to the Florida Keys for sunset. You've been sending us many e-mails with questions for Sarabiskota, and we thought this might be a good time to answer some of those. The first question comes from a second grade teacher named Anne Gilbertson. She shares the same home town as most of Sarabiskota—Bismarck, North Dakota. Anne would like to know where you got the name Gator Mikey."

"I can answer that," said Jessie. "I've got this huge Teddy bear about eight feet tall that's in my bedroom, and all my friends love it. His name is Mikey. When we were trying to come up with a name for the gator, Doc suggested it, and everyone loved it."

"That's interesting," said Jan. "Here's the next question from Hae-Ryun Park, all the way from Pusan, South Korea. It's for Mike. How did you get started doing your Elvis impersonations?"

Sarabiskota laughed. Mike said, "My parents loved Elvis a lot, so I've been singing the songs since I was really little. When I had to come up with a Halloween costume in the first grade, I dressed up and acted like Elvis. My whole class loved it, and it kinda took off from there."

"Here's a question from Megan White in West Jordan, Utah. Megan wants to know what place in Florida you'd like Gator Mikey to go that he hasn't already visited?"

"Panama City," Kari answered. "I hear they have beautiful beaches."

"Jacksonville," said Kevin. "I'd like to see their football stadium."

"Daytona Beach," said Nick. "I'm a huge NASCAR fan."

"Weeki Wachee Springs," Mike answered. "Elvis spent some time there and they have live mermaids swimming around."

"I'd like to see that myself," said Jan. "How about you, Prez?"

"I'd have to say Tallahassee. I haven't visited there before, and I'd like to see the Capitol and Florida State University and spend some time with Governor Trust."

"Thanks, Prez. We have time for one more question. This also comes from North Dakota. The Hooooshka triplets from Mandan want to know if they can borrow Gator Mikey if you ever get him under control again."

Prez smiled and answered this one. *"When* we get Gator Mikey under control again," he said, "I'd love to have Gator Mikey visit North Dakota and other places too."

Soon Gator Mikey was flying over a small key named Bahia Honda Key.

"Bahia Honda Key!" Gator Mikey exclaimed. *"Bahia honda* means *deep bay* in Spanish, and Bahia Honda Key has a deep channel on its west end. Bahia Honda Key is known for its rare plants, its beautiful beach, and its wonderful state park. It also has one of the rarest insects in the world, the Miami butterfly. The question is: Which of all the Florida keys is the largest? Is it A, Key West; B, Key Largo; or C, No Name Key?

"You know I'll repeat the question and sing a little more of my favorite Beach Boys song so you can think about the answer."

When he was finished singing, he said, "The answer is B, Key Largo. It's about 33 miles long with an area of approximately 15 square miles. Now, I wonder, is anyone smarter than me?"

"I'm smarter than a flying gator!"

"Where do you think I'm headed next? To Key West for sunset, of course. Where am I going after that? Well, I'll give you a hint: **Dot and Dash."**

Gator Mikey flew on to Key West in the twilight as the Gulfstream III followed. On the way, Prez got a call.

"Hello, Prez. This is the President. I hope you don't mind if I got your cell phone number from Governor Trust."

Prez was shocked and almost speechless. "N-n-no, Mr. President. It's such an honor to be speaking to you."

Prez's friends immediately stared at Prez when they heard he was talking to the President. They could tell this was one of the most exciting moments for Prez **EVER!**

"It's an honor for me to be speaking to you, Prez. Say, I'm headed your way in Air Force One. I have to pick up Governor Trust in Tallahassee. We won't be able to land in Key West; their airport is too small so we'll have to land in Miami. We should be there in less than two hours. I'd like to meet you and your friends at the Miami Airport if it's all right with all of you."

"Sure, Mr. President. We'd all be honored!"

"If you'd like, you and the rest of the Sarabiskota crew can chase Gator Mikey in Air Force One for awhile—assuming Gator Mikey keeps flying."

"I'm sure everyone would love to do that, Mr. President."

"I'll see you in a few hours then. I'll call the pilot and make the arrangements. Could I talk to Chad's mom and Jan Alcorn, please?"

"Sure. Thanks, Mr. President. Bye."

"Bye, Prez."

Gator Mikey circled Key West as the whole world witnessed the spectacular sunset. For the next several hours, the flying gator put on a music and light show like they'd never seen in this party town before. The people and tourists of Key West, always ready for a good time, were having the time of their lives. In the meantime, the Gulfstream III headed for the Miami International Airport for the rendezvous with the President of the United States.

After the Gulfstream III landed, several Secret Service agents riding in three carts took Chad's mom, Jan, Justin, and Sarabiskota to a special area where Air Force One was parked. When they arrived,

the President and Governor Trust welcomed them all on board.

This was a huge thrill for everyone, but Prez was in seventh heaven. As the President was taking them on a tour of Air Force One, he said, "You kids are so smart, you probably already know about the first President to ever fly in a plane."

"I believe it was Teddy Roosevelt," Prez answered. "He was no longer President at the time, though. Franklin D. Roosevelt was the first President to fly while he was in office."

"That's exactly right," the President said admiringly. "Now, I think we should get in the air and fly over to Key West. I'm anxious to see Gator Mikey in action. I've got lots of things to talk to you about on the way. How's that sound?"

"GREAT!"

"Excellent," said the President. "Let's get going."

13

At 6:59 a.m. on Monday, the extremely popular FOX & Friends morning program was about to go on the air. The shows' stars walked onto the set, each of them carrying several sheets of paper.

"Ten seconds, everyone!" the director yelled. "Alisyn, you've got cake on your face! Brian, straighten your tie! Gretchen, quit yawning! Steve, there's little hope for you! Three seconds, two, one—cue the theme music ..."

"Good Monday morning, everyone! I'm Gretchen Johannson here with Brian Stillspeed and Steve Goocy. Alisyn Cantaloopa is over there standing behind the news podium. We've got some huge Gator Mikey news to tell you about this morning, especially if you didn't stay up all night like I did."

"That's right," Brian continued. "As everyone in the world knows, one of the most unbelievable stories *ever* broke on Saturday morning. Most of us followed Gator Mikey the entire weekend as he flew all over Florida. As I went to bed late last night, the amazing flying gator was circling Key West. He was singing and putting on an incredible light show."

Steve said, "There were some HUGE developments that took place last night after the Key West spectacular. If you went to bed, you probably missed them. Gator Mikey left Key West at around 1:00 a.m. and flew to several more locations overnight. As you can see by looking at this live picture on your television screen, Air Force One has now joined the other aircraft chasing Gator Mikey around Florida."

"And the President's on board," Alisyn noted. "Along with Governor Trust of Florida and all of the Sarabiskota kids we've gotten to know the past few days."

"That's right," Brian said. "We understand Chad's mother and a news reporter and cameraman are also on board. We're actually going to do a live interview with some of the people on board Air Force One in just a couple of minutes."

"Before that interview," Gretchen continued, "we want to catch you up with some of the highlights from last night. Now, we know many of you have enjoyed trying to solve Gator Mikey's clues. If you can solve them, they tell you where Gator Mikey's flying next. Well, we're going to show you the clues

for the five places Gator Mikey visited after he left Key West last night. After that, we're going to show you an edited video of Gator Mikey's actual visits to those places. Some of you may want to mute your TV sets and look away during these next five minutes if you want to try to solve the clues on your own. All right. Here we go. First, we're going to put the five clues up on your television screen."

Alisyn read the clues out loud:

1. Dot and Dash

2. Second choice for the location of the University of Florida

3. The middle name of the first President who was also the son of a President

4. The Munchkins of the *Wizard of Oz* lived here

5. A gentle breeze

"OK," Steve said when Alisyn was finished, "now we're going to show you the slightly edited footage from Gator Mikey's visits last night. Here we go ..."

Ft. Myers! This is Ft. Myers! For 50 years

this was the winter home of Thomas Edison, the greatest inventor in the world. Did you know Edison nicknamed his first two kids Dot and Dash after the words used way back in the days when they still communicated with the telegraph? This is your question: Who was Edison's famous neighbor when he lived here? Was it A, Henry Ford; B, John Wayne; or C, Walt Disney?

"The correct answer is A, Henry Ford. He was the founder of the Ford Motor Company and the father of the modern assembly line. Do you realize Ford's neighbor, Edison, took out patents on 1,093 inventions during his lifetime? He even invented the phonograph and the first talking doll.

"Lake City! Lake City had a much cooler name before it was Lake City. What was that name? Was it A, Candytown; B, Airconditionville; or C, Alligator?

"The correct answer is C, Alligator. Lake City was named Alligator, but it wasn't directly named after my relatives and me. It was named after Chief Alligator, the chief of the Seminole Indian village that was once located here. The name of the town was changed from Alligator to Lake City because many people thought the name *Alligator* wouldn't exactly encourage too many new people to move here. That's not nice!

"Quincy! Quincy is a small town once known as the richest small town in the United States because it had so many millionaires. It's named after John Quincy Adams, the sixth President of the United States. In the 1920's, a local banker here told some of the people in the town to invest in a little company that soon became a HUGE company. The people that listened to him became rich. What company did they invest in? Was it A, Coca-Cola; B, Hershey's chocolate; or C, Mattel toys?

"The answer is A, Coca-Cola!

"This is **Venice!** Venice was the winter quarters of the Ringling Brothers and Barnum & Bailey Circus from 1960 until 1992. There was even a famous clown college here. Venice is now known for something else. In fact, it's known as the capital of the world for what particular thing? Is it A, clown paintings; B, purple sea shells; or C, sharks' teeth?

"The correct answer is C, sharks' teeth. Millions of these fossilized teeth wash up on the beaches near Venice. They even have a Shark's Tooth Festival in the spring.

"Zephyrhills! Zephyrhills is best known for what? Is it A, gold jewelry; B, water; or C, the jelly bean museum?

"The correct answer is B, water. The man who picked this place to build a town after the Civil War chose it because of its good water."

Gretchen said, "That should catch us up with the 16 locations Gator Mikey has visited so far, beginning with Gainesville. When Gator Mikey left Zephyrhills 45 minutes ago and began flying northwest, he gave this clue: **the county seat of the county whose name spelled backwards has a Christmas theme."**

Steve said, "I know where he's headed. I already checked the 67 county names."

"Good for you," said Brian. "But right now it's our pleasure to go live on board Air Force One. Hello, everyone!"

"Good morning!" everybody replied enthusiastically. They were all standing close together in the Main Conference Room on board Air Force One.

"Mr. President, this is Gretchen Johansson. Maybe we could start with you. How much fun is this for you?"

"I actually feel like a kid again just being around

these young people with all their enthusiasm. Sharing the Gator Mikey experience with all of them last night was fantastic! The light show the flying gator put on must have been one of the most incredible things ever witnessed on Planet Earth!"

Gretchen asked, "Governor Trust, how has this experience been for you?"

"I would have to agree with the President. How much better can it be than this? I also like the fact that the whole world's focused on Florida for such a fun thing, and I get to fly on Air Force One."

"Prez, this is Steve Goocy. I know you got your name because you want to be President someday. This must be extra special for you."

"No doubt. This is significantly better than my wildest dreams!"

"Kevin, this is Alisyn Cantaloopa. We understand some of you have figured out a possible pattern to the places Gator Mikey's visited so far. You've even predicted the places he's going to visit today."

"I think we might have figured out a possible pattern, but Gator Mikey probably has lots of surprises in store for us."

"Do you want to share anything you figured out?" Alisyn asked.

"It's probably more fun if you figure things out yourself," said Kevin.

"KT, this is Brian. What's been your highlight so far?"

"Hi, Brian. Everything has been a highlight for me, but being here on Air Force One with the President and Governor Trust is hard to beat!"

Brian said, "Well, we want to invite all of you to New York City to be on our show when this is all over. Hopefully, you can bring Gator Mikey along."

"That would be great!"

"Thank-you!"

Alisyn said, "We hope to talk to you again next hour. Right now, it looks like Gator Mikey and you are approaching the capital city of Florida, Tallahassee!"

Gator Mikey approached Florida's two Capitol buildings. He swooped down to an altitude of less than 50 yards above the newer, taller building as tens of thousands of people cheered on the ground below him. Seconds later, the crowd waved and applauded loudly when they saw Air Force One approach from the southeast.

"Capitol buildings!" Gator Mikey called. "I'm flying over the two Capitol buildings here in Tallahassee! The smaller building is the old Capitol. It was completed in 1845, and two wings and a dome were added after that as the state grew in population. The other building is the newer, 22 story Capitol, which was finished in 1977. My next question: Which state has the tallest Capitol building? Is it A, Louisiana; B, Florida; or C, Nebraska?

"Of course, I'll repeat the question and give you ten more seconds to think about it after that."

Gator Mikey repeated the question and sang the beginning of Florida's brand new state song for ten

seconds. After that he said, "The correct answer is A, Louisiana. Their Capitol is 34 stories high, a total of 450 feet. That's still not as high as the doors were back at the Vehicle Assembly Building at Kennedy Space Center. Now you know exactly what to say if you got this question right! Say it **NOW!**"

"I'm smarter than a flying gator!"

"Very good!" Gator Mikey cried out. "Now, I'll be staying here for half an hour or so, and you'll never guess where I'm flying next. I'll give you a hint: **Geronimo!**"

"This is Shonda Knight from WCTV Channel 6 in Tallahassee. I'm here in Capitol Square this morning with Professor Tim Leno, a history professor from nearby Florida State University. Professor Leno knows a great deal about our local and state history. Professor, right now we're in the midst of a huge crowd, watching a magnificent colorful alligator flying over us. He's singing the Florida State Song in his beautiful Elvis voice. We've got Air Force One with the President and Governor Trust and Sarabiskota on board and all those jets and helicopters in the air nearby. As you watch this all take place, are you reminded of any other big historical events that may have occurred here in the past?"

"Yes, Shonda, but certainly nothing as spectacular as this. Of course, just seeing a blue and orange gator flying over our city reminds us all of the many great football games between our beloved Florida State Seminoles and those annoying Gators from Gainesville."

Shonda giggled. "That's for sure."

"Other than that," Professor Leno continued, "the first Christmas ever celebrated in North America was celebrated about a mile southeast of where we're standing right now. That took place at a campsite of the Spanish explorer Hernando de Soto in 1539."

"Really? That's interesting. Anything else?"

"Sure. When Tallahassee became a United States territory in 1821, the territory's first nonmilitary governor was William Duval. He actually succeeded Andrew Jackson, who was the military governor for just a short time. Anyway, Duval had a beautiful daughter named Elizabeth, who liked to flirt with the young men who lived around here. Two of those guys fought a duel with pistols over Elizabeth right here in Capitol Square."

"What happened?"

"Well, fortunately neither of the men were very good shots and they weren't hurt seriously. It turned out Elizabeth really didn't care for either of them much. She just liked the attention."

"Fascinating, Professor. Do you have any more?"

"Sure. Way back in 1826, we had a big royal wedding right here in Tallahassee. George Washington's great grandniece married a prince, Prince Murat. The prince just happened to be the nephew of a pretty famous historical character, Napoleon Bonaparte, the Emperor of France."

"Thanks, Professor Leno. I have to admit I never liked history, but this has been very interesting— Wow! Gator Mikey just flew right over us!" Shonda had to yell to be heard. "Professor Leno, do you have one more as Gator Mikey flies away from us?"

"Sure. None of us will ever forget the whole presidential election of 2000 that played out right here in Tallahassee. For several weeks, we weren't sure whether it would be Bush or Gore as our next President of the United States. Tallahassee was a pretty crazy place back then, but there were no flying gators."

"Speaking of that flying gator, he's now singing

a Beach Boys favorite of mine."

Gator Mikey was singing "I Get Around" as everyone was dancing and singing to the music.

"This song would make an excellent theme song for Gator Mikey!" Professor Leno yelled over all the loud singing. "He definitely gets around."

"Good one, Professor!" said Shonda. "Well, this is Shonda Knight singing and dancing along with Gator Mikey and thousands of others in Tallahassee!"

A few blocks away, on the campus of Florida State University, head football coach Bobby Boodeen was humming the Beach Boys' song as he watched his television. Coach Boodeen was in his office, but he wasn't working on new football plays.

His old blackboard was filled with Gator Mikey clues, Gator Mikey questions and answers, and the names of the places Gator Mikey had visited. He walked over and looked out his window as Gator Mikey approached. "Daw-gum it!" he yelled. "Couldn't those Sarabiskota kids have built a flying tomahawk or something!"

When Gator Mikey was out of sight, Coach Boodeen walked back over to his old blackboard. He picked up a piece of chalk and wrote the word **Geronimo** on the board. He also added the word **Capitol** to his list of places Gator Mikey had stopped and asked questions. Just for the fun of it, he circled the first letter of each of the seventeen place names—beginning with Gainesville and ending with

Capitol.

"Wait a second!" Coach Boodeen exclaimed. "It can't be this simple! Gator Mikey's playing some sort of alphabet game with me. He hasn't used any letter of the alphabet more than once! Hmmm, I wonder if there's a pattern here? I may not be smarter than a daw-gum flying gator, but I'm not that dumb either!"

16

Gator Mikey flew almost straight west out of Tallahassee, singing an old song from the 1960's called "The Wanderer." The flying gator had changed some of the lyrics, though:

> I'm the type of gator
>   Who likes to roam around,
> I'm never in one place,
>   I roam from town to town,
>
> I'm asking tough questions,
>   Don't stick around too long,
>
> Then I take off again,
>   And fly to another town,
>
> Cause I'm a wanderer,
>   A gator wanderer,
>
> I roam around around around around,

Cause I'm a wanderer,
A gator wanderer,
I roam around around around around...

In the Main Conference Room on board Air Force One, the President, Governor Trust, Sarabiskota, and Chad's mom were busily doing research on the Internet.

Prez asked, "Has anyone found anything about Geronimo that might be connected to Florida?"

"Bingo!" the President exclaimed. "I've got something here. This is interesting. Geronimo was a famous Apache medicine man, not an Indian chief like I thought. It says here he was captured along with his band of warriors in 1886 at a place in New Mexico called Skeleton Canyon. Then he was sent to Florida to a fort in St. Augustine to be imprisoned. After that, some business leaders in Pensacola arranged for Geronimo to be sent there. Geronimo ended up being jailed at Fort Pickens in Pensacola."

"That's it, Mr. President!" Jessie exclaimed. "Good job! We're going to Pensacola."

"Yeah, way to go, Mr. President!" Doc added.

Nick looked puzzled. "Why did the business leaders in Pensacola want Geronimo at Fort

Pickens?"

"Geronimo was famous," the President answered. "When he refused to be put on a reservation in the 1870's, he and his band raided New Mexico, Arizona, and Northern Mexico for a long time before they were caught. The newspapers had written about Geronimo's exploits over the years. The businessmen in Pensacola thought Geronimo would be a good tourist attraction."

"They wanted to use a famous prisoner as a tourist attraction?" Kevin asked in disbelief.

Governor Trust grimaced. "Yup, it seems like my state will do just about anything to attract more tourists."

"It must have worked," said the President. "It says here they had over 450 people visit in one day and the people were sad to see Geronimo leave."

"Where did he go?" Kari asked.

"It doesn't say here," the President answered.

"Look!" Chad said excitedly. "You're going to like this, Prez. It says Geronimo rode in the Inaugural Parade of President Teddy Roosevelt!"

"Too cool!" Prez said.

Mike asked, "Why do people yell **Geronimo** when they jump out of planes and things?"

"I've got that right here," Governor Trust replied. "It started with a six foot eight inch paratrooper from Ft. Benning, Georgia, named Private Aubrey Eberhardt. Back in 1940, they were training to do a particularly dangerous jump out of an airplane. The night before, the men watched a movie about Geronimo to help them get over their nervousness. Even though the private was known to be brave, his friends gave him a rough time about being really nervous about the jump. To help prove he wasn't nervous, Private Eberhardt told his friends he was going to yell **GERONIMO!** when he jumped out of the plane the next day."

"Did he?" KT asked.

"Yup, he did," Governor Trust replied. "Then he followed it with a big Indian war whoop."

"This is fantastic stuff," said Chad.

"Here's something interesting about Pensacola," Mike noted. "I always thought St. Augustine was the first European settlement in the United States, but I guess that's not right. Pensacola was settled in 1559 and St. Augustine was settled six years after that in 1565. Pensacola wins for first European settlement."

"What's the deal?" Doc wanted to know.

"Well," Mike explained, "that first settlement in Pensacola was hit by a hurricane and it was practically wiped out. After two years, everyone had left and no one tried to resettle the area for more than 100 years."

"But St. Augustine has been settled *continuously* since 1565," KT noted, "so they get the credit for being first in the history books."

Nick looked a little confused. "I think I get it."

"Hey look!" the President exclaimed.

"It's the Blue Angels!" Kevin shouted excitedly as the six beautiful blue and yellow jet aircraft flew off the right side of Air Force One.

Everyone glanced at the President, who was trying to act like he knew nothing about this. "What?" he said. "The Blue Angels are stationed in Pensacola and they happen to be in town. Their commanding officer called a while ago, and he asked if they could escort us into Pensacola. How could I turn them down?"

The Blue Angels flew in delta formation, smoke on, leading Gator Mikey, Air Force One, and all the other aircraft into Pensacola. Gator Mikey saw smoke trailing from the Blue Angels' F/A -18 Hornets and he decided to do the same. Soon, blue and orange smoke was coming from the flying gator's tail end.

"Wow!" said Prez. "This just keeps getting better and better."

Once they got to Pensacola, the Blue Angels showed everyone some of their stuff as they put on a brief air show for the huge crowd gathered on the ground. Gator Mikey decided to put on a little air show himself. With orange and blue smoke trailing behind, Gator Mikey spelled *I Love Pensacola!* in the air. The crowd loved it, as did the billions watching on television around the world.

"Pensacola!" Gator Mikey cried out as he flew above the throng assembled in the Pensacola area. "The name **Pensacola** comes from the name of the Indian tribe that once lived here. The next question is: What does that name mean? Is it A, bubbly soft drink; B, alligator people; or C, long-haired people? As always, I will repeat the question and give you ten seconds to think about the answer."

Gator Mikey repeated the question and sang ten seconds of the song "Earth Angel." Then he said, "The correct answer is C, long-haired people. Now, you know what to say if you got the question right. At the count of 3! 1 ... 2 ... **3!**"

"I'm smarter than a flying gator!"

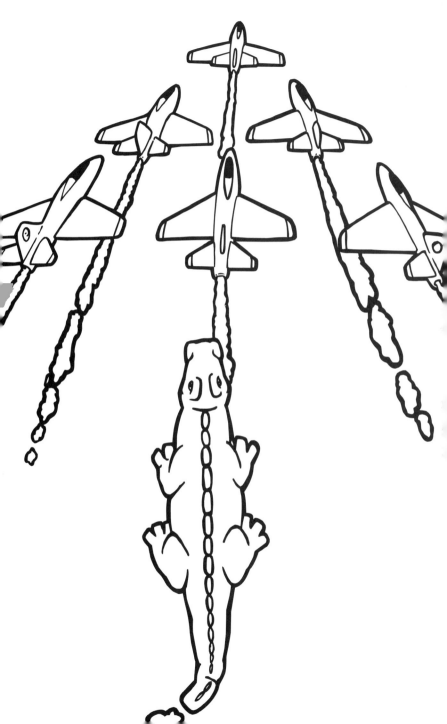

"Where am I flying next? I'll give you a hint: **February 22, 1959!**"

Doc studied the information on her computer screen. "Hey, Nick," she said excitedly. "I *know* you're going to like *this.*"

"Like what?" Nick asked as he quickly walked over to take a look at Doc's computer screen.

Doc pointed and said, "February 22, 1959, is a huge day for NASCAR fans like you."

Nick studied the information for several seconds. "Oh, my gosh!" he shouted. "February 22, 1959, was the day they had the first Daytona 500 at the Daytona International Speedway! We're headed to Daytona Beach!"

Nick ran over to the nearest window on Air Force One and yelled, "Thank you, Gator Mikey! We're going to Daytona!"

The President gave Nick a high five as everyone celebrated with Nick.

"Excuse me," said the President. "I'm going to see if we can get some pizza and beverages in here for our big celebration."

The President went to his office and made a phone call. After that, he went to talk to the chef about making some pizza.

"Nick," said Prez as he continued to research the first Daytona 500, "from what I'm reading here, the first race must have been pretty awesome."

"What do you mean?" Nick asked.

"After 500 miles of racing, it came down to a photo finish. There were actually three cars in that photo, but one car had been lapped. Lee Petty's and Johnny Beauchamp's cars were the other two."

"Who won?" Nick wanted to know.

"Johnny Beauchamp ... at first," Prez explained. "But then they studied the photos and the film taken during the race. After three days they changed their minds. Lee Petty was declared the winner by just two feet."

"That's incredible—but kind of a bummer for Johnny Beauchamp," said Nick.

"How fast did the winning drivers race back then?" Kevin inquired.

"Petty averaged 135.5 miles per hour for the whole race," Prez answered. "This is pretty interesting stuff, Nick—for a sport where they just drive around in circles endlessly."

Nick made a face at Prez.

Prez continued. "Lee Petty got about $19,000 for winning that first Daytona 500. Last year's winner, Jeffie Gordon, got nearly two million."

"Unreal," said Chad.

The President walked back in the room with a mischievous smile on his face. "Nick, you have a phone call. I'll put it on the speaker phone in here for you."

"Who is it?" Nick asked.

"A friend of yours," the President said, about ready to burst.

"Hello?" Nick said.

"Hello, Nick! This is one of your big fans, Jeffie Gordon!"

"Really? Jeffie Gordon? I'm one of *your* biggest fans!"

"Nick, our whole NASCAR 24 team loves you guys. We're all keeping track of you and Gator Mikey and the President, Governor Trust, and your Sarabiskota friends."

"You are?"

"You bet. Everyone's trying to figure out where Gator Mikey's going next, and we're trying to answer all of Gator Mikey's questions. It's been a blast!

Who knew history and geography could be so much fun? I can proudly say I've gotten ten of the eighteen questions correct so far."

"That's excellent, Mr. Gordon."

"You can call me Jeffie."

"Thanks, Jeffie."

"You're welcome, Nick. By the way, my pit crew and I think we know where Gator Mikey will fly after Daytona Beach."

"Where?"

"Well, like Gator Mikey likes to do, I'll give you a hint: **Coacoochee.**"

"Coacoochee? How do you spell that?"

"C-o-a-c-o-o-c-h-e-e. Anyway, Nick, I know you're about ready to have a little pizza party on board Air Force One. Before I go, my 24 team and I would like to invite you and your friends to be part of our honorary pit crew at the next Daytona 500 if you'd like. Maybe Sarabiskota can even take a look under the hood of my car and make it go as fast as Gator Mikey."

"Really? The Daytona 500?"

"Really, Nick. How's that sound?"

"Fabulous! Thanks so much, Mr. Gordon—Uh, Jeffie!"

"You're welcome, Nick. Say hi to everyone else for me. Good-bye."

"Good-bye!"

Gator Mikey approached Daytona Beach where tens of thousands of cheering people were waiting. The flying gator swooped down to a low altitude and flew over the world's most famous beach, then he approached Daytona International Speedway.

"Daytona Beach! The World's Most Famous Beach!" he called. "Daytona Beach was named after Mathias Day, who bought the land around here in 1870. Auto racing started on the beach, but now it takes place at the famous speedway down below. One of the most famous racers on the beach ever was a man by the name of Malcolm Campbell from England. The King of England knighted him back in 1931 when he was able to break the land speed record. Right here on Daytona Beach, Malcolm was able to travel one mile in his automobile in less than how many seconds—after he got a running start? Was it A, two seconds; B, 12 seconds, or C, 22 seconds?"

Gator Mikey repeated the question. After that, he made the sounds of a speeding race car for ten seconds.

"The answer is B, 12 seconds. Malcolm broke the speed record of 246 miles per hour that day. The land speed record now is over 760 miles per hour!

"If you answered the question correctly, I'll bet you know what to say!"

"I'm smarter than a flying gator!"

"Tremendous! Now, where am I flying next? I'll give you a little hint: **1903 Gatormobile."**

"This is Jan Alcorn, on board Air Force One. We're headed up the East Coast of Florida right now. I'm here in the Main Conference Room with the President of the United States, Governor Trust, Chad's mom, and Sarabiskota. As you can tell, there's a beehive of activity going on.

"Over here we have the President, Jessie, and Mike working together. Jessie, what's going on?"

Jessie said, "Well, a few minutes ago, the President found the photo of the Gatormobile from 1903 that Gator Mikey was talking about in his clue. It's right here."

"What exactly is that?" asked Jan.

"It's a photograph of the 18th governor of Florida, William S. Jennings," Jessie explained.

Jan described the photo to the TV audience. "As you can see," she said, "he's riding in a chariot with a live alligator pulling it. It's called the Gatormobile."

"The picture was taken at the Old City Gate in St. Augustine," the President added. "It looks like Gator Mikey's headed to St. Augustine for sunset."

"Excellent," said Jan. "Now we're walking over here to where KT, Doc, Prez, and Governor Trust are working. What are you four finding out?"

Governor Trust said, "We're researching St. Augustine. We just found out they have an alligator farm there. That may have something to do with Gator Mikey picking St. Augustine."

KT said, "They've got a huge crocodile there named Maximo. He's about 15 feet 3 inches in length. It says he was born in 1971, hatched on a crocodile farm in Australia."

"They've got albino alligators, crocodiles, birds, emus, and even kookaburras there," Doc added.

"What's a kookaburra look like?" Jan wanted to know.

"It's a big Australian bird," Prez said, showing her a picture of one on his computer screen. "They make a distinct sound like a human being laughing."

"That's fascinating," said Jan. "I hope I can see

a kookaburra sometime and hear that sound. Now, let's go over to where Chad's mom is working with Kari, Chad, Nick, and Kevin. Mrs. Renner, are you enjoying yourself?"

"More than you can ever imagine."

"Kari, what are you researching?"

"Well, Jeffie Gordon talked to Nick on the phone and gave him a clue to where he thought Gator Mikey was going to fly after he left Daytona Beach. We were just checking that clue out. It turns out Jeffie and his team were right."

"What was the clue again, Nick?" Jan asked.

Nick spelled it out, "C-o-a-c-o-o-c-h-e-e. Coacoochee."

"Coacoochee," Jan repeated. "Interesting word. What is it?"

"Actually, it's more like *who* is it?" said Kevin. "Coacoochee was a great Seminole Indian chief who was jailed in a Spanish fort called Castillo de San Marcos in St. Augustine. You'll never believe how he escaped."

"How?" Jan asked.

"It wasn't easy," said Chad. "The only way out was a little window more than 15 feet off the ground. It was too small for a man of Coacoochee's size to squeeze through."

"But that wasn't the only problem," Kevin added. "There was a guy posted outside the prison cell all the time."

"Were there other prisoners in the cell with Coacoochee?" Jan asked, getting more curious by the moment.

"Yes," said Chad. "But there's another problem. There were bars on that little window."

"We've only got a few seconds," said Jan, anxious to find out how Coacoochee escaped. "Aren't you going to tell our viewers and me how he finally escaped?"

"There's not enough time," said Nick. "I guess they'll have to look it up themselves."

"All right," said Jan. "This is Jan Alcorn about to look up that answer— and reporting from on board Air Force One."

18

"Good morning! I'm Steve Goocy. It's Tuesday morning, Day 4 of Gator Mikey's Amazing Adventure, and this is FOX & Friends!"

"And Gator Mikey is at Walt Disney World this morning," Brian Stillspeed announced. "Right now, you're watching a live shot of the famous gator flying about 50 feet above Adventureland at Walt Disney World in Orlando, Florida. My own kids are going to be *so* excited when they see Gator Mikey on TV this morning. They love Walt Disney World, and they love Gator Mikey!"

"The same for my kids," Gretchen Johannson added. "If you went to bed last night, you probably don't know that Gator Mikey visited three more locations in the dark after he left St. Augustine. We will catch you up on those visits in just a moment."

Alisyn Cantaloopa yawned. "I stayed up and watched the whole thing. I wouldn't have missed it for anything."

Steve asked, "Alisyn, would you like to give our

viewers a little more information before you start snoring away?"

"Oh, sure. Gator Mikey arrived in Orlando about 25 minutes ago. The Disney World people have decided to open up the park one hour early this morning, at 8:00 a.m. That would be in about 52 minutes. Right now, you can see some of the thousands and thousands of people starting to converge on the Orlando area in their cars—"

"WOW!" Gretchen exclaimed. "There's Gator Mikey flying over Cinderella's Castle in Fantasyland!"

"Unbelievable!" said Steve. "The Magic Kingdom has never seen this kind of magic!"

"No doubt," Brian said. "We've got Walt Disney World. We've got Gator Mikey flying overhead singing one of my favorite songs, 'It's a Small World After All.' It simply doesn't get much better than this!"

"The song seems to be so pertinent for a flying gator with Gator Mikey's abilities," Steve added.

"Gator Mikey seems to have changed the lyrics somewhat," Gretchen noted. "Let's listen in for a few moments as he sings with that beautiful Elvis voice of his."

It's a world of kind people,
   A world with a rising sun,
It's a world with a flying gator,
   A world of fun,

There's so much that we share,
   That it's time that we care,
In this small, small world ...

Brian wiped tears from his eyes. "That was beautiful," he said. "I love that song."

"Brian," said Steve, "we're getting word now that Air Force One has landed at the Orlando International Airport. The President, Governor Trust, and Sarabiskota are on their way to Walt Disney World at this moment."

Gretchen said, "As we continue to watch Gator Mikey fly over Walt Disney World, this might be a good time to talk about his three visits last night. Those of you who didn't stay up last night and like to solve the clues yourselves may want to mute your televisions and look away for about five minutes as we show the clues and the edited version of Gator Mikey's visits. We'll begin right now by putting the three clues on the screen for you."

Brian read the clues to the television viewers:

1. Sebastian the Ibis's team's nickname
2. Indian word meaning *laughing waters*
3. Cow Ford

"Now," Steve said after the clues were displayed, "here we go with the edited tape of Gator Mikey's visits last night."

"Hurricanes! Miami is the home of this beautiful University of Miami, whose teams are nicknamed the **Hurricanes!** Their mascot is an ibis because an ibis is the last animal to take shelter before a hurricane. *Hurricanes* is a good nickname for a Florida university because many hurricanes seem to be attracted to Florida. This is my question: Throughout history, out of every ten hurricanes that have made landfall in the United States, how many have hit Florida? Is it A, two out of every ten; B, four out of every ten; or C, five out of every ten?

"The correct answer is B, four out of every ten. Would you believe 279 hurricanes hit the United States mainland since 1851; 113 of those hit Florida!

"Umatilla! Umatilla was named after an Oregon town with the same name. The town's name is an Indian word meaning *laughing waters*. Every October, Umatilla has a big festival. What's the name of that festival? Is it A, The Florida Comedy Festival; B, The Florida Alligator Festival; or C, The Florida Black Bear Festival?

"The correct answer is C, The Florida Black Bear Festival. Umatilla is the gateway to the Ocala National Forest. Lots of black bears live in the area.

"Jacksonville! Jacksonville was named after the territorial governor of Florida who became the seventh President of the United States. It was called *Cow Ford* at one time because it's the narrowest crossing of the St. Johns River for many miles. Here's the question, a geography question: Jacksonville is directly south of what major city in the United States? Is it A, Cleveland; B, New York City; or C, St. Louis?

"The correct answer is A, Cleveland."

"We're back live," said Steve. "And Gator Mikey's causing quite a ruckus as he flies over the animals at Kilimanjaro Safari. Look at those big gators!"

"Now Gator Mikey's swooping down as he approaches MGM Studios," Brian pointed out. "He seems to be dropping down over Mickey Avenue."

"Walt Disney World!" Gator Mikey called out.

"This is the greatest place on earth! I've got a Walt Disney question for you. Walt Disney had another name for his famous mouse before his wife, Lilly, suggested *Mickey*. What was that name? Was it A, Mikey Mouse; B, Mortimer Mouse; or C, Milton Mouse?

"I'm going to repeat the question and then sing the theme song of the *Mickey Mouse Show* while you're thinking about the answer."

Gator Mikey did just that. When he was done, he said, "The correct answer is B, Mortimer Mouse. Now, everyone knows what to say if they got the question right!"

"I'm smarter than a flying gator!"

"That was terrific! Right now I'm going to fly over Walt Disney World and sing my favorite Disney songs. Where will I go after that? Well, I'll sing you a little song before I leave this wonderful place at noon. That will help you figure out my next destination. Isn't that *nice* of me?"

Gator Mikey's visit helped Walt Disney World shatter their one day attendance record by eleven o'clock that morning. At noon, the famous flying gator hovered over Spaceship Earth at Epcot Center.

"Where am I going next?" Gator Mikey called. "Listen to my favorite Disney song and you'll probably figure it out ..."

In a huge garage at the Pocono Racetrack in Pennsylvania, Jeffie Gordon, his mechanics, and his pit crew were watching the television with great interest. They'd all just finished singing the popular song "A Whole New World" with Gator Mikey.

Soft-hearted mechanic Will Volk loved that song. He actually had tears streaming down his cheeks. **"Hey!"** he said in his deep voice, wiping the tears from his face with a towel. "Gator Mikey replaced the word *new* with *nice* in the last line of the song."

Jeffie Gordon ran over to his computer and said, "I'll do a quick Google search and see if there's a town in Florida with the word *nice* in it!"

"Got it!" Will Volk said excitedly, beating Jeffie to the punch. "It's right here near Fort Walton Beach on the panhandle!"

Back in the office of head football coach Bobby Boodeen, the coach had added another portable blackboard to his office.

"Look, Gator Mikey," he said out loud to himself. "I know where you're headed next—but then what? You're running out of letters of the *daw-gum* alphabet! What are you going to do with **'X'?"**

On his portable blackboard, Coach Boodeen had written the names of every town in the United States he could find whose name began with the letter 'X':

Xanadu, Utah
Xavier, Kansas
X Crossing, Montana
Xenia, Kansas
Xenia, Iowa
Xenia, Ohio
Xenia, Colorado
Xenophen, Tennessee
X-prairie, Mississippi

Coach Boodeen started yelling at his TV set. "So, where are you going next, Gator Mikey!? Are you going to leave Florida or what!? And where do they come up with a *daw-gum* word like *Xenophen* anyway? *Xavier's* not such a bad name for a town – but *Xenophen?*"

Air Force One was right behind Gator Mikey as were countless other jets of all sizes. Gator Mikey was flying north northwest toward the panhandle. On board, everyone was having the time of their lives after a most memorable morning at Walt Disney World.

"Mr. President and Governor Trust," said Jessie. "Thanks for the Walt Disney World experience. I've been there before, but never with the President and governor. It's even more fun with you guys."

"No problem, Jessie," the President said. "I had more fun than you did."

"Yeah, it was our pleasure," added Governor Trust.

"Hey, look!" Nick said as he glanced at the Weather Channel. "There's a huge band of thunderstorms developing off the West Coast of Florida, extending all the way up into Georgia."

"Wow!" Kevin exclaimed. "It's HUGE!"

"We'll be through that area before it causes any problems," Prez assured them.

The whole world watched as Gator Mikey flew over Choctawhatchee Bay and approached the town of Niceville, Florida. By this time, thousands of people had gathered near the center of town. Gator Mikey circled around the town's huge water tower as the people cheered!

"Niceville!" called Gator Mikey. "Niceville is a great name for such a fine, pleasant, wonderful community as this! Niceville has not always had such a nice name, though. Take a guess what Niceville was called before 1910. Was it A, Boggy; B, Yucksville, or C, Muddtown?

"I will repeat the question and then show you my *twisty wisty* double somersault maneuver while you're thinking of the correct answer."

Gator Mikey repeated the question. After that, he showed off for the crowd, performing a flying maneuver that no other aircraft in the world could match. The crowd cheered loudly!

When he was done, Gator Mikey said. "That was fun! By the way, the correct answer is A, Boggy. The name came from a nearby sandy-bottomed bayou called Boggy Bayou. There's even a festival here in October called the Boggy Bayou Mullet Festival!

"If I go 1 ... 2 ... **3!**, do you know what to yell?"

"I'm smarter than a flying gator!"

"Phenomenal! Where am I going next? **X-tra! X-tra!** You'll know pretty soon!"

As Gator Mikey flew south southeast, Jeffie Gordon said, "Oh, no! Gator Mikey's flying toward that huge band of thunderstorms!"

"Daw-gum it! What are you doing?" Coach Boodeen yelled at his television.

"Prez, can Gator Mikey survive if he flies through that?" KT asked.

"I can't watch!" Jessie said, hiding her eyes.

"It makes no sense! Why doesn't he fly around that huge storm?" Will Volk said anxiously.

"Our pilot says we have to fly around it," said the President. "We'll all pray for Gator Mikey."

Gator Mikey flew right into the massive band of thunderstorms. Within a matter of seconds, he disappeared completely amidst a massive onslaught of wind, lightning, thunder, and rain like Florida hadn't seen in years!

20

Gator Mikey totally disappeared. There were no radar sightings. The weather was much too bad for there to be any visual sightings from any aircraft. The GPS signal being transmitted by the flying gator was no longer being received by Prez. The whole world watched anxiously, worried that Gator Mikey had gone down into the ocean off the West Coast of Florida.

"Please help Gator Mikey," Tyler Hooooshka prayed back in Mandan, North Dakota.

"I refuse to believe it's over for Gator Mikey," the Queen of England told one of her aides in Buckingham Palace.

Two year-old Katrice Kern held her Teddy bear tightly while watching the television at her home in Bismarck with her parents. "He's got to be OK!" she cried.

"When the going gets tough, Gator Mikey gets tougher—or something like that," said Coach Boodeen in his office in Tallahassee.

"Yikes!" Sir Ian yelled at his TV in Brisbane, Australia.

On board Air Force One, which was approaching McDill Air Force Base in Tampa for refueling, no one was even close to giving up.

"We'll get back in the air before the storms hit us," said the President. "Don't worry. I know Gator Mikey's OK."

"Alligators love weather like this, don't they?" Nick said, trying to make himself feel better.

"Sure they do," KT answered quickly.

"Prez, can Gator Mikey survive a lightning strike?" Kari asked.

"I'm almost sure," Prez replied.

Air Force One got back in the air and flew south along the edge of the storm. Suddenly, the pilot of a Coast Guard helicopter flying off the coast near Anna Maria Island yelled, "We have Gator Mikey in our sights! He's coming out of a huge thunder cloud. He seems to be OK! He's currently flying south about 20 yards above the stormy waves of the Gulf of Mexico. Mr. President, we are equipped to send you a live video feed."

"Please do!" the President answered anxiously. "We'll send your video and audio on to the media."

The whole world cheered when they saw the live pictures of Gator Mikey on their television screens a few minutes later.

"Gator Mikey's heading straight for Siesta Key!" KT exclaimed.

"He is!" Chad cried. "He's only 12 miles north of there right now!"

Everyone watched excitedly as Gator Mikey continued flying south, just off the West Coast of Florida, barely above the ocean's waves.

"Oh, WOW!" the Coast Guard pilot yelled 15 minutes later. "I hope everyone's enjoying this as much as we are! Gator Mikey is flying through the most beautiful rainbow you've ever seen. He now appears to be slowing down and approaching a big gold building down below us! Oh, my gosh! There's a huge Super Bowl XL logo painted on top of the building! Gator Mikey appears to be going in for a landing! He is! He's landing right on the letter **'X'!"**

The next few weeks before school started were a whirlwind of activity for Sarabiskota and Gator Mikey. After the world's most famous gator got a major tune up, there were many special appearances around the country. The world couldn't get enough of the Gator Mikey story.

School started in late August, but Sarabiskota still managed to get together at least two weekends each month for Gator Mikey events. Mostly, they appeared at college and professional football games.

Their first game was a Florida Gators college football game in Gainesville. Their second one was in Pittsburgh for a Steelers home game. Wherever Sarabiskota appeared with Gator Mikey, the huge crowds of football fans loved it.

At the end of the year, Gator Mikey had his own Christmas special on TV. He sang Elvis Presley's famous holiday songs while flying over some of the most beautiful areas of the country. It eventually became the most popular Christmas special *ever.*

The new year arrived and Sarabiskota and Gator Mikey were chosen to be Grand Marshals of the Rose Bowl Parade in Pasadena, California. Sarabiskota led the parade riding in two beautiful, red convertibles. Gator Mikey flew proudly overhead.

One month later, they were all special guests at the Super Bowl in Miami, Florida, where the Pittsburgh Steelers played the Tampa Bay Buccaneers. Sarabiskota even got to watch the game from the sidelines near the Steelers' bench. Gator Mikey helped televise the game as he circled slowly above the stadium. The Steelers won the game 31-28!

On February 17, the President, Governor Trust, and Sarabiskota were having a terrific time down by the racetrack before the Daytona 500 automobile race began. All the drivers and mechanics and pit crew teams were anxious to meet Jeffie Gordon's honorary pit crew. Nick was in heaven.

As race time approached, the announcer yelled, "And now, to give us the most famous six words in racing, I'll turn it over to the most famous gator on the planet by far! Now flying over this wonderful Daytona

International Speedway, **it's Gator Mikey!"**

The enormous crowd went wild! Gator Mikey flew over the racetrack to thunderous applause, proudly flying an American flag behind him.

"Ladies and gentlemen!" Gator Mikey announced proudly. **"Start your engines!"**

ABOUT THE ARTIST

Dave Ely is a self-taught artist with many talents. Besides illustrating books, he does custom wood carvings, bone sculptures, steel sculptures, and paintings. Many of his works depict a Western or wildlife theme.

Dave grew up in Bismarck, North Dakota, and he continues to live and work there. He draws inspiration from the people and wildlife in that area.

Dave recently placed first at the National Taxidermy Contest in the reptile category; he placed second in the world for that same entry. He has also done a life-size bear carving and an eagle carving for the movie *Wooly Boys*.

To view some of Dave's work or to contact him, go to: **www.elywoodcarving.com**

ABOUT THE AUTHOR

When he was teaching fifth and sixth grades in North Dakota, Kevin Kremer began writing stories with his students. It was largely due to their encouragement that he wrote his first book, *A Kremer Christmas Miracle,* as a Christmas gift to his students and family. After that book was published, Kremer just kept on writing.

Kremer loves sports. The Pittsburgh Steelers and Oklahoma Sooners are his favorite football teams, but he's rapidly becoming a fan of some of the Florida college football teams since he moved there from North Dakota. Kevin has never met a Steelers fan he didn't like.

Dr. Kremer has started a writing/publishing company to help people with writing projects of any kind. To contact him regarding writing or publishing projects, school author visitations, or to purchase books, go to:

Web site: **www.snowinsarasota.com**
e-mail: **snowinsarasota@aol.com**